The past could not be undone, and both of them knew it.

Heather's laughter drew Daniel's gaze away from Monica and down the hillside. The sound touched a deep and empty corner of his heart. Strange. He hadn't known the corner was empty until he'd met Heather.

"Monica, it's time to tell her who I am."

He heard her tiny intake of breath, but he didn't look toward her.

"You know I'm right. We can't go on pretending I'm just Mr. Rourke, an old college buddy. She should know who I am."

She touched his arm, drawing his gaze first to her fingertips, then to her face. "Once we tell her, your life will never be the same."

"It won't ever be the same anyway."

Dear Reader,

February is the month of love...glorious love. And to commemorate the soul-searching connection between a man and a woman, Special Edition has six irresistibly romantic stories that will leave you feeling warm and toasty from the inside out.

Patricia Thayer returns to Special Edition with *Baby, Our Baby!*—a poignant THAT'S MY BABY! tale that promises to tug the heartstrings. Ali Pierce had one exquisite night with the man she adored, and their passionate joining brought them the most precious gift of all—a child. You won't want to miss this deeply stirring reunion romance about the tender bonds of family.

Cupid casts a magical spell over these next three couples. First, an intense bodyguard falls for the feisty innocent he's bound to protect in *The President's Daughter* by award-winning author Annette Broadrick. Next, *Anything, Any Time, Any Place* by Lucy Gordon is about a loyal bride who was about to marry her groom, until a mesmerizing man insisting he had a prior claim on her heart whisks her away.... And a forbidden desire is reignited between a lovely librarian and a dashing pilot in *The Major and the Librarian* by Nikki Benjamin.

Rounding off the month, celebrated author Robin Lee Hatcher debuts in Special Edition with a compelling story about a man, a woman and the child that brings them together—this time forever—in *Hometown Girl.* And finally, *Unexpected Family* by Laurie Campbell is a heartfelt tale about a shocking secret that ultimately brings one family closer together.

I hope you enjoy all our captivating stories this month. Happy Valentine's Day!

Sincerely,

Karen Taylor Richman
Senior Editor

Please address questions and book requests to:
Silhouette Reader Service
U.S.: 3010 Walden Ave., P.O. Box 1325, Buffalo, NY 14269
Canadian: P.O. Box 609, Fort Erie, Ont. L2A 5X3

ROBIN LEE HATCHER

HOMETOWN GIRL

Silhouette®

SPECIAL ▼ EDITION®

Published by Silhouette Books

America's Publisher of Contemporary Romance

SILHOUETTE BOOKS

ISBN 0-373-24229-8

HOMETOWN GIRL

Copyright © 1999 by Robin Lee Hatcher

This edition published by arrangement with Harlequin Books S.A.

® and TM are trademarks of Harlequin Books S.A., used under license. Trademarks indicated with ® are registered in the United States Patent and Trademark Office, the Canadian Trade Marks Office and in other countries.

Printed in U.S.A.

ROBIN LEE HATCHER

discovered her vocation as a writer after many years of reading everything she could put her hands on, including the backs of cereal boxes and ketchup bottles. However, she's certain there are better plots and fewer calories in her books than in puffed rice and hamburgers. A past president of Romance Writers of America, Robin is the author of over twenty-five novels. Her books have won numerous awards, including the Heart of Romance Readers' Choice Award for Best Historical, a Career Achievement Award for American Romance from *Romantic Times Magazine,* and the Favorite Historical Author Award from *Affaire de Coeur.* She was a finalist for the prestigious RWA RITA Award in 1992. For her efforts on behalf of literacy, Laubach Literacy International named their romance award "The Robin."

In those rare moments when she isn't working on a new book, Robin and her husband, Jerry, like to escape to their cabin in the mountains of Idaho with their border collie and Shetland sheepdog. Hobbies are nearly nonexistent since she sold her first book, but she enjoys the occasional golf game (don't ask about the scores!), loves movies (both old and new) and live musical theater and is a season-ticket holder with the Idaho Shakespeare Festival. She also loves to spend time with her two daughters and three young grandchildren.

She invites readers to find out more by sending a #10 SASE to P.O. Box 4722, Boise, ID 83711-4722.

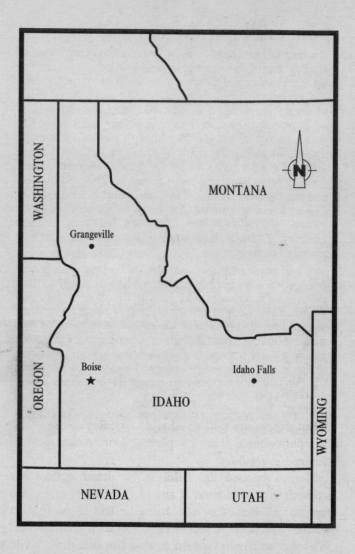

Chapter One

Monica stood on the sidewalk outside of the Reading Nook Bookstore and Coffee Shop, trying to muster the courage she needed to walk inside. It would take plenty of determination, for through those doors she would find Daniel Rourke. A man she'd thought she would never see again.

Maybe she shouldn't do it. Maybe she should just forget it.

But she couldn't. She had to do this. Because the tearful confrontation with her parents four weeks ago had changed everything.

Monica pressed the palm of her hand against her stomach. She wondered if she had the fortitude to face him, to tell him what she knew he had to be told. It would have been so much easier to send him a letter. Why did he have to return to Boise at this time, while she was still grappling with her confusion and hurt, not to mention her guilt?

She glanced longingly toward her car at the far end of the jam-packed parking lot. She could *still* send him a letter, she told herself. She didn't have to tell him in person.

But, of course, she did. He might have walked out on her eleven years ago, breaking their engagement and her heart, but that hadn't given her the right to keep such a secret from him.

She knew that now.

Maybe she'd always known it.

But only recently had she been forced to acknowledge that wrong. Her whole world had been shaken by the revelation of her adoption. In an instant, old truths were no longer true. As a result, she'd found herself questioning everything else in her life. She had trusted her mom and dad implicitly. No matter what else happened, she'd always known she could turn to them, that she could trust and believe in them. But it turned out they had lied to her. So now who or what could she trust?

While searching for the answer to that question, she'd realized she'd done something even worse to Daniel Rourke: she'd never told him he had a daughter. She'd never told him about Heather.

Drawing a quick breath, she stepped forward and pushed open the bookstore door, moving quickly inside before she could chicken out. She saw the table set up in the center of the huge store, but she couldn't see Daniel. He was hidden behind a crowd of fans, waiting to buy his blockbuster book.

She wandered through the aisles, glancing frequently toward the table, wondering how long she would have to wait for the crowd to clear. Suddenly she found herself with an unobstructed view of him, and her heart nearly stopped.

Daniel.

She'd seen him on TV during the past years, of course, and she'd seen his photos in the magazines. But seeing him in person was different.

Impossible though it seemed, he'd grown more handsome through the years. He wore his black hair shorter now. His jaw was clean shaven. He was trim, tanned, fit. And he wore his success with an easy confidence that was tangible, even from across the bookstore. He was no longer the student who had been her steady boyfriend throughout her college years, the young man who had been her first and only lover, the person she'd lived with for more than a year and planned to marry. That Daniel had still been a boy in many ways. This Daniel appeared mature, virile, perhaps even a little dangerous.

The ladies must love him, she thought—and felt an uncomfortable sting in her chest.

Monica was well aware of Daniel Rourke's success. It would have been nearly impossible *not* to know since his photo and byline had popped up so often in newspapers and magazines, especially in the last few years. Daniel had been on the fast track as a hotshot newspaper reporter in Chicago for a decade now. But his star had really taken off as he'd followed and reported on the sensational Henderson murder trial. He'd even won some awards for his coverage.

When the trial and its immediate aftermath were over, he'd written his book about it. *And The Rich Kill,* by Daniel Rourke, was now number eight on the bestseller list, and he'd become a household name. His face had appeared in every major magazine. He'd also been interviewed on all the top morning news programs.

Monica hated to admit it, but she'd read all the articles about him, caught all the talk shows when he was on. She told herself it was only because she was interested in the trial and its results, not because of Daniel.

Surely that was true.

He's never married, she thought as she watched him hand another book to a fawning young woman with bright red hair and a come-hither smile.

She wondered why he'd never married. But then, she knew why, didn't she?

She knew why all too well.

Daniel Rourke hated sitting in a bookstore, autographing copies of his book. He hated it more than having a root canal. But thank goodness, this one was the last he would have to endure. His tour ended here in Boise, and none too soon. He was exhausted after four weeks and twenty-two cities.

Of course, his publisher hadn't originally scheduled Boise, Idaho, into the tour. That had been done at Daniel's request. He'd decided months ago he needed a breather. He was extending his sabbatical from the newspaper for another three months. He was going to stay in his dad's old house, maybe do some fishing and camping. He was going to try to relax—if he could remember how. It had been a long time since he'd even tried.

He scribbled his name on the title page and handed it to the grinning middle-aged woman across the table from him.

"It's so exciting to have you here, Mr. Rourke," she gushed. "I had no idea you were a Boise native until I read the article in the paper this morning. Your parents must be very proud."

"My parents are deceased." Not that it was any of

the woman's business, but Daniel was learning there was little privacy in his life these days.

"Oh, I'm so sorry." She flushed with embarrassment. "I... I..."

"It's all right. It's been a long time."

The woman clutched her copy of his book close to her ample bosom and hurried away.

Cathy Monroe, the bookstore manager, stepped unobtrusively to his right side, whispering, "Is there anything you need, Mr. Rourke? I could get you coffee or a cola or—"

"No, I'm fine, Cathy." He smiled at her, saw her overeager smile in return. "Thanks anyway." He hoped she didn't read more into his politeness than was intended. He'd lately discovered how willing some women were to do just that. It was amazing what a difference a high six-figure book deal could make in a man's social life, once the facts were published in every newspaper and scandal sheet in the country.

On his left side, Allison True, his publicist, slid another book in front of him, already open to the title page. He glanced up at the person across the table.

"And who should I sign this—" he began. The words died abruptly in his throat.

"Hello, Daniel."

For a moment, his voice wouldn't work. Finally, her name came out. "Monica?"

He shouldn't have been surprised to see her, but he was. Or maybe it was the way seeing her again made him feel. Unsteady. Off balance. As if he'd been rudely awakened from a sound sleep and wasn't quite sure where or even who he was.

She offered a tentative smile. "It's been a long time."

A *long* time? It had been a *lifetime*. "Eleven years," he managed to say.

"Yes." She gestured toward the stacks of books. "You've done well for yourself."

"I've done all right." But what he wanted to say was, How about you, Monica? What have you done with yourself? Are you married? Do you have that little house and white picket fence like you always wanted? Are you happy?

She looked incredible. She must be happy.

If anything, Monica Fletcher was more beautiful than he'd remembered. She still wore her golden blond hair long and curly. Her brown eyes were still the color of chocolate truffles—her favorite candy in college. She wasn't as skinny as she'd been when she was twenty, but she wore the few extra pounds well. They'd added some lovely curves.

He cleared his throat. "Should I sign this to you?"

"Please."

He tried to think of something clever to write. But what did one say to an ex-lover, to a former fiancée, to a woman who had been his sunshine until he'd driven her away? Finally he just scribbled his name.

As he closed the book, she said, "Daniel, I was wondering if we might talk when you're finished here. You don't have a flight to catch, do you?"

"No." He held out the book to her. "As a matter of fact, I'm staying in Boise for a few months."

"Oh, I didn't know." She seemed flustered. "Could we..." she began, then glanced at Allison, obviously wondering who the woman was. "Could we go for coffee or something to eat when you're done?"

He had to admit he was surprised Monica wanted to spend any time with him. After all, they hadn't parted on the best of terms. Before he'd moved out of their apartment, their fights had turned bitter and caustic. They'd said a lot of things to wound each other. They'd both been pretty good at it, but he'd been the champion. He'd always known her most vulnerable points, and he'd used them against her.

He'd hurt her. Intentionally.

It wasn't something of which he was especially proud.

"I won't keep you long," Monica continued, her gaze flicking to the publicist again.

It was time for an introduction. "Allison, meet my—" What was he supposed to call her? He settled for, "Old college friend, Monica Fletcher." He paused, glancing toward her left hand, but his book was in the way. "*Is* it still Fletcher?"

"Yes."

He wasn't about to analyze the way her answer made him feel. "Monica, this is Allison True. She works for my publisher. It's her job to get me all the places I have to be, on time, looking good and feeling organized. She's been a real trouper on this tour."

"It hasn't been all bad," Allison said as she offered her hand to Monica. "I've worked with many more temperamental and demanding authors than Daniel." She glanced at him and chuckled. "Although you *have* had your moments," she teased, then returned her gaze to Monica. "It's a pleasure to meet you, Miss Fletcher. Boise is a lovely city. I'm not surprised Daniel wanted to come back here for a well-deserved rest."

Monica offered a tight smile in response, then glanced behind her. "I'd better get out of the way and let Daniel sign the rest of these books." She was no longer speaking to him, but to Allison. "I'll just browse until he's finished."

Daniel watched her walk away and wondered what had caused her to seek him out. Monica Fletcher was no groupie, no fortune hunter, he was certain of that. He had a vague suspicion she would have preferred that same root canal he'd been thinking about earlier rather than coming here to see him.

So why had she come?

"Mr. Rourke, I'm so excited to meet you. I've already read your book…"

Reluctantly he returned his attention to the reader across the table, smiling automatically. "And you want this autographed to…"

The restaurant lounge was busy. In the opposite corner, a television was tuned to a basketball game, and voices rose and fell in response to baskets made and missed. While waiting for their drinks, Monica and Daniel munched on chips and salsa and tried to act casual about this meeting after so many years.

"Do you like living in Chicago?" Monica asked.

"It's got its good and bad points." Daniel shrugged. "A lot different than here, that's for certain."

"Boise's changed a lot since you went away."

"Yeah, it has. I couldn't believe the traffic, getting from the airport to the bookstore."

Monica hooked a loose strand of hair behind her ear. "You've never been back in all these years?"

She already knew the answer. In the beginning, she'd watched for him, longing for the phone call that would have announced he was returning…to her. Later, she'd dreaded it. And finally, she'd accepted, for better or worse, he wasn't ever going to call, wasn't ever going to return.

"No," he said in answer to her question.

Hardly above a whisper, she asked, "Why now?"

His steel gray eyes darkened as he met her gaze. "Wish I hadn't come?"

Yes. "No."

Leaning back in his chair, he raked the fingers of his right hand through his hair. "To tell you the truth, Monica, I'm tired. I needed a change, a rest. So I'm extending my sabbatical from the paper until September. I'm going to stay in Dad's old house. Fix it up a little. Maybe I'll sell it before I go back to Chicago. But while I'm here, I'm going fishing, camping, hiking. You know, all the outdoor stuff Idaho is famous for. Who knows what else? Maybe I'll go bungee jumping."

Earlier, she'd thought he sounded wistful. Now he sounded weary and maybe a bit flippant. It was on the tip of her tongue to ask him if he was happy, but the waitress arrived with their drinks.

While Daniel paid for the margaritas, Monica breathed a silent sigh of relief. She was glad for the interruption, glad she hadn't asked him about his personal happiness. It wasn't why she'd come to see him today.

As if he'd read her thoughts, Daniel said, "Why did you ask me here, Monica?"

Her mouth went dry. The moment had come.

"I don't think it was for old time's sake," he added with a wry smile.

She took a sip of her drink, then drew a deep breath as she set her glass on the table. "I have something to tell you, but I'm not sure how to do it."

He raised one eyebrow. Curious. Nothing more.

"It's about Heather. My daughter."

"Your *daughter?*"

She nodded. Her gaze dropped to the table where she

was slowly shredding a cocktail napkin with her finger-tips.

"I guess I assumed, since your name is still Fletcher..." He let the sentence die unfinished.

"I'm not divorced," she supplied. "I never married."

"Oh."

This was much harder than she'd anticipated it would be.

She glanced up, met his gaze again. "Heather will be eleven years old in September," she said softly, then waited.

She could almost see the wheels in his head turning, could almost hear him adding and subtracting and coming up with the only possible sum. His eyes widened a fraction. His black eyebrows drew together in a frown. His back stiffened as he leaned slightly forward.

"What are you saying, Monica?" It was a needless question.

She answered it anyway. "Heather is your daughter."

He stared at her, unmoving, his expression suddenly closed and unrevealing. She imagined it was the same neutral mask he wore in his work as an investigative reporter.

"I'm sorry, Daniel," she whispered as her hands closed around her margarita glass in an attempt to still their shaking.

"You're sorry? You're telling me you gave birth to my child almost eleven years ago and never bothered to tell me. And you're *sorry?*"

Monica closed her eyes. As if it was yesterday instead of more than a decade ago, she recalled their final argument. His voice had been angrier then, yet much the same. *Just don't go trying to trap me into marriage by pulling that pregnancy thing like Jennifer did to Tony. It won't work on me. We're finished.*

She lifted her gaze. "You would have hated me."

"Hated you? What the hell are you—"

"It would have ruined all your plans. You wanted other things. Remember? You decided you didn't want a marriage and family."

Daniel struggled to rein in his anger as he stared across the table at Monica. She seemed much too poised, considering what she'd just told him. As if she didn't realize her disclosure was earthshaking. As if she didn't know her revelation had hit him in the gut with the force of a .44 Magnum.

A child. A daughter. And already half grown.

He stared hard at the woman seated opposite him and wondered, briefly, if this had to do with money. Maybe she'd decided it was time to cash in on his success. The old Monica wouldn't have been so calculating, but how did he know what she would do now? Time had to have changed her, just as it had changed him.

"Why now?" he demanded gruffly.

Monica paled. Something akin to pain flashed in her eyes, then disappeared. "It's a long story. Let's just say I realized I had to tell you the truth. I would have written, but then I heard you were coming to Boise, so I waited. I thought it might be better in person."

"When can I meet her?"

"I hadn't thought—"

"That I'd want to meet her?" Sarcasm deepened his voice.

"No... I..." She paused, drew a quivery breath, then said, "I didn't know what you'd want, Daniel. I don't know who you are anymore."

Her words echoed his own thoughts of moments before.

Years ago, they'd been in love. Two college kids with their lives stretching out before them. They'd had big dreams and unlimited expectations. More than once in the years that had passed since then, Daniel had regretted breaking up with Monica. But she was a hometown girl who had wanted white picket fences, a house on a tree-shaded street and babies. Daniel had wanted fame and fortune, bright lights and big cities.

"Daniel?"

"What?"

"You didn't want to be trapped by an unplanned pregnancy. Remember?"

He swore softly. It was true. That's what he'd told her. He'd meant it, too. Still, to have kept this a secret all these years...

"Is that what you thought you could do, Monica? Trap me into marriage? Is that why you got pregnant?"

He said it to hurt her. When he saw her flinch, he figured he'd succeeded. It didn't make him feel any better, but he wasn't sorry for it.

She shook her head and mouthed the word, "No."

His voice still terse, he asked, "What does she... What does Heather know about me?"

Monica's eyes grew misty. She shook her head again.

"She must have asked who her father is."

"Yes."

"And?"

"I told her I would explain things when she was older."

Daniel cursed as he stood. "I want to meet her."

Monica stood, too. "Of course."

"When?"

She looked at him for a long time before answering. "Whenever you like, Daniel." She held out her hand, offering him a business card. "I wrote my home number on the back."

He took the card. "I'll call you tomorrow." He turned and strode out of the restaurant lounge.

After Daniel disappeared through the archway, Monica sank onto her chair, feeling too drained and shaky to maneuver her own way through the crowded bar.

"Would you like another drink?"

She glanced up at the waitress, then down at the nearly untouched margarita before her. "No. Thank you."

"Sure thing. Give a holler if you change your mind." The woman moved to another table.

Monica looked around the lounge. A bluish haze of cigarette smoke floated above the patrons' heads. In the opposite corner, the television was now turned off, the game apparently over. Music played in the background.

She would have to tell Heather about Daniel. She had to tell her daughter the truth.

And heaven only knew what would happen next.

Daniel hadn't been inside his dad's old house since shortly after Richard and Stephanie Rourke died in a car accident during Daniel's sophomore year in college. It seemed strange to be in it now.

He stood in the middle of the living room, wondering how a house could shrink. He didn't remember the place being this small.

The rental management people had replaced the carpet twice over the years. They'd painted the interior about a half-dozen times. About five years ago, some renters had put a hole through the wall dividing the living room and kitchen. Daniel had paid the bill for those repairs, and apparently he'd gotten his money's worth. He couldn't tell where the hole had been.

He walked into the kitchen, half expecting to see Stephanie, his dad's fourth wife and Daniel's favorite stepmom, standing at the stove. Stephanie Rourke had always been happiest in the kitchen, whipping up something delicious for her husband and stepson. She'd been quite the gourmet cook. He hadn't appreciated it back then. He would now, but it was too late.

Daniel felt a sting of longing for the past. It caught him off guard. He'd been glad to shake off Boise's dust when he'd left for Chicago all those years ago.

A daughter. He had a daughter.

The thought hit him suddenly and left him winded.

A daughter. Heather. Heather what? Fletcher?

Anger returned. He'd bet a year's wages her last name was Fletcher since Monica hadn't bothered to tell anyone he was the father. Least of all Daniel himself.

How could she have done this to him? How could she just decide to shut him out?

Maybe the girl wasn't his.

But he knew better. Monica wouldn't have been unfaithful to him back then and she wouldn't lie to him now. If she said Heather was his child, then she was.

You didn't want to be trapped by an unplanned pregnancy. Remember?

He leaned against the door of the forty-year-old refrigerator, fighting the urge to pound his forehead repeatedly against the cool white surface. He'd come to Boise to relax, to find some answers, to decide what it was he wanted to do with the rest of his life.

Well, having a daughter would certainly affect the rest of his life. That was for sure.

Chapter Two

The jangle of the telephone caused Monica to jump. She stared at the offending contraption as if it were evil incarnate.

"I'll get it, Mama," Heather called from upstairs.

"No!" she shouted quickly, grabbing for the receiver. "I've got it." She lifted it to her ear. "Hello."

"Monica?" her mother's voice came across the wire. "Are you all right, dear? You sound strange."

She pressed her free hand against her chest in an attempt to quiet her racing heart. "I'm fine, Mom."

"Dad and I didn't see you in church this morning. I was afraid Heather might be sick again."

Monica's head was beginning to pound. Maybe *she* was sick. "No, we...we just overslept."

"Well, that's a relief. We were hoping you two might join us for a barbecue this afternoon. It's such a beautiful spring day. Your father can't wait to fire up the grill."

A beep interrupted her mother, announcing another incoming call. Monica was relieved; she wasn't ready to tell Ellen Fletcher that she'd gone to see Daniel yesterday.

"Hang on a minute, Mom," she said quickly, then tapped the switch-hook with her index finger. "Hello."

"Monica? It's Daniel."

Oh Lord! She wasn't ready for this, either. She hadn't talked to Heather. She'd put it off all morning.

"Monica?"

"Yes. Yes, I'm here. Just a moment while I get off the other line."

"Sure."

Again she depressed the switch-hook. "Mom, I've got to take this call. We'd better take a rain check on that barbecue. I'll call you later."

"But, dear—"

She hung up on her mother.

"I'm back," Monica said into the receiver, trying hard to sound normal. She didn't succeed. She could hear the uncertainty in her voice.

Daniel got right to the point. "I thought about this situation all night. I think it would be best if I met Heather before we tell her who I am. Give her a chance to get to know me. What do you think?"

"If…if that's what you want."

"It is."

"Okay."

He cleared his throat. "This afternoon?"

"That would be fine." Monica closed her eyes a moment. The headache was intensifying. "Why don't you come for an early dinner? Say four o'clock?"

There was a lengthy silence on the other end of the line. "What are you going to tell her about who I am?"

"I...I'll tell her you're an old college friend. Just like you introduced me yesterday. She's probably seen your photo in the newspaper. Be ready for questions and lots of them."

"Right." Another pause. "I got your address out of the phone book, but you need to tell me how to get there."

"We're in a subdivision off Overland, west of Maple Grove. It isn't hard to find."

"I'll be there at four."

"Okay." Her voice broke on the word.

Daniel hung up without saying goodbye. Monica assumed he was still angry. And could she blame him if he was?

Yes, she answered silently, summoning a bit of anger for herself. She *could* blame him. *He* was the one who had decided he didn't want marriage, that a career was more important to him. *He* was the one who had said he wasn't ready to settle down and have a wife and family. *He* was the one who had walked out on her, breaking her heart along with their engagement.

Her anger didn't last long. All her arguments were true, but they still didn't excuse her for the secret she'd kept from him. Daniel should have known he had a daughter. He should have been given a choice. Monica hadn't given him one.

Drawing a deep breath, she walked out of the kitchen and stood at the bottom of the stairs. Music—if one could call it that—blared from beyond her daughter's bedroom door.

"Heather!" she called.

No answer.

Rubbing her forehead with her fingertips, she climbed to the second floor. She rapped on the door. When she still didn't get a reply, she opened it. Heather was lying on her back on the floor, eyes closed. Her black hair, worn in pigtails, curled in twin circles on the carpet.

"Heather," Monica said loudly.

Her daughter opened her eyes.

"Mind if I turn this down?" She stepped toward the stereo and fiddled with the knobs until she found the right one.

When she looked at her daughter again, she had to swallow a gasp. It was a long time since she'd thought how much Heather resembled Daniel. She'd come to see her child as an individual, unique, not looking like anyone but herself. But now Monica saw the resemblance again. Their gray eyes. Their aquiline noses. The stubborn jut of their chins. The olive tone of their skin.

How could Heather not guess Daniel was her father the moment they met? Was she making a mistake not to tell the whole truth before he arrived?

"Did you need something, Mama?"

She forced a smile. "We've got a guest coming over for dinner. I've got to go to the store. Want to come along?"

"Sure." Heather hopped up from the floor as if she hadn't undergone an emergency appendectomy only a month before. "Who's coming?"

"An old college friend of mine. His name is Daniel Rourke."

Heather grinned—a smile just like her father's. "A man? Gee, Mama. That's pretty cool."

Monica resisted the urge to pull her daughter into a tight hug. Her life was spinning out of control, and she didn't know how to stop it.

Daniel steered the rental car up close to the curb and braked. He cut the red convertible's engine, then turned his head to look out the window.

Monica's home was a two-story, brick-and-frame house in a newer, upscale neighborhood. The deep green lawn was freshly cut. Flowers of every variety and hue bloomed alongside the curving sidewalk that led from the driveway to the front door. Three young aspens applauded Daniel's arrival with fluttering leaves.

As he got out of his car, he wondered what Monica did for a living. The card she'd given him was generic, listing only the company name, address and phone number. Her name and position with Solutions, Inc., weren't printed on it. Judging by this subdivision and her home, it looked as though she'd been successful at whatever she was doing.

She hadn't needed him, that much was clear. She'd succeeded in providing for herself and her daughter—*their* daughter—without his help or interference. No wonder she'd never told him about Heather.

Bitterness left a sour taste in his mouth as he headed up the walk.

The door opened before he reached it. A bright-eyed youngster stepped into the sunlight. Her black hair was captured in two pigtails with yellow ribbons that matched her short set. "Hi," she greeted him. "You must be Mr. Rourke."

Heather. His daughter.

Daniel wasn't often caught speechless. His profession didn't allow him that luxury. But this was one of those rare times when his mind drew a blank.

"Mama said you went to college with her. How come we've never met before?"

"I live in Chicago," he managed to reply.

Except for her long hair, looking at Heather was like

looking at an old photograph of himself at the same age. She was tall for ten, thin and wiry. Her right knee had been skinned a while back, the scab just beginning to disappear.

Heather watched him, one eyebrow raised higher than the other, her gaze frank and curious. A duplicate of an expression Daniel himself often wore.

If he'd had any doubts about his paternity, they would have been dispelled now. The resemblance was uncanny.

"Hello, Daniel."

He looked up to find Monica standing in the open doorway.

"Welcome to our home," she added softly.

"Thanks."

Heather grabbed hold of his hand. "Come on in. I want you to tell me all about my mom when she was in school." She dragged him past Monica, through the living room and kitchen and into the family room.

Daniel's instincts as a reporter didn't completely fail him. In those few brief moments, he managed to notice many details about Monica's home. It had a warm, cozy feel. Lots of windows, letting in plenty of sunshine. Springtime colors—mauve, teal, soft yellow, sky blue. Uncluttered, yet lived in. Two oak-and-glass carousels held video tapes, including what appeared to be all the Disney movies available, both old and new. There was a neat stack of CDs beside the stereo; he couldn't read the titles or the names of the artists. He wondered if Monica's taste in music had changed. She'd always liked country. He still preferred classic rock and roll.

"Look," Heather said. "I dug out Mom's old yearbooks. I found your picture."

The green-and-gold high school yearbook lay open on a glass-and-wood coffee table. Faces from the Borah

Lions' senior class stared up at him. His was in the center of the page.

He almost laughed at the sight. Had he ever been that young? Fifteen years felt more like fifty.

"Mine's worse."

Daniel glanced at Monica and experienced a deep sense of nostalgia. Fifteen years melted away like magic, and they were both eighteen again, eagerly awaiting graduation and college and the bright glorious future. Monica looked the same now as she had then. Only prettier. No wonder he'd fallen in love with her that summer.

Surprise, then wariness entered her brown eyes, breaking the spell. She moved away from him. When she spoke, her voice seemed strained. "I hope you still like fried chicken. It's Heather's favorite."

"Really?" Daniel looked at the girl. "Mine, too."

Heather grinned. "Do you like dogs?"

"Hot dogs?"

"No, silly. *Real* dogs."

He grinned back at her. "Sure do."

"Then come meet mine. Her name's Cotton." She took his hand again. "Do you have a dog? I've had Cotton since she was a puppy."

Monica watched as her daughter led Daniel out the back door. As soon as it closed, she sank onto the sofa and covered her face with her hands. She was shaking all over. Nerves, she told herself, but honesty made her wonder if it wasn't something much more. Something she hadn't felt in a long, long time.

Desire?

She sat up straight. Her hands fell away.

Good grief! What was she thinking? She hadn't seen or heard from Daniel in over eleven years. Whatever she'd once felt for him was nothing more than a memory.

But it was the memory of their lovemaking that had popped into her head when Daniel looked at her just moments ago. And the sudden spurt of longing that swept through her had caught her totally unawares.

Monica had intentionally avoided serious relationships with men during the past decade. Partially it was because she'd stopped believing in happily ever afters when Daniel walked out. But it was also because she'd seen plenty of stepparent situations hurt the children involved. She hadn't wanted that for Heather. Her daughter had come first from the moment she'd held the squalling, red-faced infant in her arms. She'd nearly forgotten what it was like to feel the strong pull of sexual attraction, to feel the sweep of need rush through her, pooling deep within, weakening her knees and making her forget reason and common sense.

Anyone but Daniel, she told herself as she stood again. By nature of his fatherhood, Daniel already had the power to rock the boat of Monica's carefully constructed life. She wasn't about to hand him another means with which to create havoc.

She walked over to the glass door that opened onto the patio. Daniel stood with his shoulder leaning against the awning post, watching as Heather tossed a Frisbee to Cotton, a white mop of a dog of undefinable breed. But it was Daniel who held Monica's gaze.

Yesterday, he'd looked the part of famous reporter and author, a man accustomed to hotel suites, limousines, publicists and all the other trappings of success. But today he looked much more like the Daniel she'd known in college. His red shirt was unbuttoned at the collar, revealing dark chest hair at the base of his throat.

Red was a good color on him. Always had been.

He laughed, and crinkles appeared at the outer corners of his eyes. The lines were new; the smile was the same.

Memories of walking hand-in-hand with him down tree-lined streets near the university flitted through her mind. She imagined the crisp smell of fall in the air as golden maple and oak leaves fluttered to the ground to crunch beneath their feet.

She blinked, surprised to find tears blurring her vision. When she could see clearly again, she found Daniel watching her through the patio door.

Go back to Chicago, Daniel. Let things be as they were.

And in his eyes, she saw the answer to her silent plea: Things aren't ever going to be the same again, Monica. They can't be.

Dinner went better than Daniel had expected. That was thanks mostly to Heather's personality. She was bright and inquisitive for a ten-year-old. At least it seemed so to him. But then, he wasn't well acquainted with many ten-year-olds. Maybe they were all like Heather.

No, he thought as he watched her clear the table in response to her mother's request. Heather was different, special.

Pride. That's what he felt when he looked at her. If circumstances were different, he might have laughed at the strangeness of his discovery. How often through the years had he told others—women especially—that he had no desire to have children, that his career came first, that there was no time in his life for a wife and children, home and family, that the ticking clock was a female thing? To suddenly find himself feeling paternal toward this little girl was at odds with all those pronouncements.

His gaze shifted to Monica. It was she who had a right to be proud. She was the one who had given birth, who had cared for and nurtured Heather alone.

All he'd done, Daniel admitted silently, was make love to a beautiful woman whom he'd adored. An enjoyable interlude. A climax. And that climactic moment had made him a father.

But it hadn't made him a dad.

Even he knew that being a dad took time, involvement, commitment.

The anger that had simmered in his chest for the past thirty hours began to cool. It wasn't pleasant, facing the truth about himself. But Daniel's profession was all about seeking the truth, and he wasn't going to let himself off the hook that easily. Like it or not, he had to accept the part he'd played in Monica's decision to keep Heather a secret. He was far from blameless. She'd had good reason for making that choice.

"Monica."

She looked at him. Uncertainty swirled in the chocolate depths of her eyes.

"She's a terrific kid. You can be proud."

A smile played at the corners of her mouth and some of the tension left her shoulders. "I am proud."

He leaned forward, and lowered his voice so only she could hear. "I'm not going to try to take over. I'd just like to get to know her. We'll go slow."

He saw the glitter of tears, watched as she blinked them away. "Thanks, Daniel."

He glanced at his watch. "Maybe I'd better go."

Monica looked relieved. "Perhaps so. Tomorrow is a school day, and I have to be up early for work."

It occurred to him as they both stood that she'd said little throughout the meal, mostly because he'd been peppered with questions from Heather. He'd failed to ask what work Monica did or much of anything else about her life during the past eleven years. Was she involved with anyone? Had she ever come close to getting married?

"Are you going already?" Heather asked when she saw Monica and Daniel walking toward the living room and the front door.

"Yeah," Daniel replied. "But I'd like to come again if you don't mind. I'm going to be in Boise for a few months."

Heather's gaze darted between them. "We'd like that, wouldn't we, Mama?"

Monica hesitated a moment, then replied, "Yes. Of course we would."

He was surprised by how much he hoped she meant it, but he didn't let on. He gave both Heather and Monica a nod and a smile. "I'll give you a call." Then he turned and went down the walk toward his car.

Three hours later, Monica lay on her bed, staring up at the ceiling. Sleep refused to come.

She kept hearing Heather's words after Daniel left. *He's nice, Mama. I like him. Don't you?*

She hadn't known how to answer then. She wouldn't know how to answer now. *Did* she like him? It seemed too difficult a question for a simple yes or no. Daniel had the power to hurt Heather. He also had the power to make the girl happy, to give her—if not a whole family—at least a father.

I like him. Don't you?

"It isn't important whether I like him or not," she muttered. "It's only important that Heather does."

She rolled onto her side and stared toward the bedroom window, which was cracked open to let in the fresh night air. A breeze caused the drapes to flutter and sway. Moonlight danced across the carpet in tempo with the gentle wind.

Suddenly it was another spring. The night of her twenty-first birthday. The night Daniel proposed to her. They'd lived together nearly a year by that time, but she'd been talking about marriage for much longer. Secretly she'd begun to fear he would never propose. She'd even understood, at least partly, his resistance to matrimony. His dad had been married four times, widowed once, and divorced twice. Daniel's childhood had been one of constant change.

But on that night in May, as they'd strolled in the moonlight, Daniel had asked Monica to marry him after graduation. It had been the happiest night of her life. So happy she hadn't listened to everything else he was saying. That he didn't want to stay in Boise. That he wasn't in a hurry to have a family.

Or maybe she'd heard and simply ignored what he'd wanted.

Is that what you thought you could do, Monica? Trap me into marriage? Is that why you got pregnant?

She rolled onto her back and stared at the ceiling once again.

"Maybe it was," she confessed in a whisper.

They'd fought so often in the months that followed her birthday and their engagement. They'd fought about everything, large and small. She'd felt Daniel pulling away from her. She'd felt her happiness being stripped away, layer by layer. Maybe, subconsciously, she'd thought pregnancy was the answer. She'd only forgotten to take the pill a couple of times, but maybe those couple of times hadn't really been an accident.

She gave her head a small shake and mentally yanked her thoughts forward in time. It didn't matter what had happened back then. She was no longer that same girl, so desperately in love. And Daniel was no longer that same boy. They had both changed a lot over the years.

Besides, it was Heather's happiness, Heather's future, that mattered most to Monica. Her own feelings about Daniel, as complicated and confused as they were, mattered not at all.

Chapter Three

The city of Daniel's birth had grown tremendously during the decade he was away. In the shadow of the mountains, the downtown area had changed more than expected. New buildings of brick and glass shot skyward. Two-way streets had become one-way streets and vice versa. Beyond downtown, subdivisions had spread to the east and west along the Boise River, and more homes and businesses had gobbled up farmland and desert sagebrush to the south.

Daniel spent Monday morning driving around, getting his bearings and the lay of the land. There were plenty of things that were familiar. Plenty more that were new and unexpected.

By noon, he felt himself inexplicably drawn to the address on Monica's business card.

Solutions, Inc., was located in one of the new downtown office buildings. Daniel parked his car in an underground parking garage, then took the elevator to the ninth floor.

The elevator doors opened into an exquisite lobby, decorated in hues of mauve and teal. The carpet was thick and squishy underfoot. The overstuffed mauve chairs were upholstered in soft leather. About twenty feet away, a reception desk sat in front of two ten-foot-high, thick glass doors. Gold lettering on that glass identified the business as Solutions, Inc.

He still didn't know what sort of solutions this company had, but whatever it was, they were good at it, judging solely by what Daniel could see here.

A young, perky-looking receptionist, wearing a telephone headset, glanced up from the paperwork on her desk and gave Daniel a welcoming smile. "Good afternoon. May I help you?"

"Yes." He strode across the lobby, stopping in front of the desk. "I'm looking for Monica Fletcher. Is she available?"

"One moment and I'll see. May I tell her your name?"

"Daniel Rourke."

She raised her eyebrows. "Oh, just like that famous newspaper guy."

"Yeah, just like him."

The receptionist pressed a button on the elaborate phone system. "Ms. Fletcher, there's a Daniel Rourke here to see you."

While the young woman listened to whatever Monica was saying, Daniel let his gaze move around the lobby once again. It reminded him just a little of Monica's living room. The colors were similar, and he thought the large vase in the corner—filled with colored ostrich feathers and dried flowers—was a duplicate of the one he'd seen in Monica's entry hall.

"Mr. Rourke?"

He looked back at the receptionist.

"Ms. Fletcher said you may go in. Do you know where her office is?"

"No. I'm sorry. I don't."

She continued to smile as she pointed. "Just go through those doors and make a right. Go all the way to the end of the hall. Ms. Fletcher has the last office. You can't miss it. There's a sign on her door."

"Thanks."

Daniel found that the inner offices were just as well-appointed as the lobby. Quality prints hung on the walls. Classic lamps adorned large desks of oak and cherry wood. Judging by how quiet it was, he suspected most people were at lunch. He wondered why Monica wasn't.

He reached the end of the hall and came to an abrupt stop, staring at the nameplate on the wood door that read: Monica Fletcher, President, Solutions, Inc.

President? Before he could knock, the door opened in front of him, and there stood Monica.

She wore her golden curls swept up in a no-nonsense chignon. Soft brown shadow colored her eyelids. Her lovely mouth was tinted dark pink. Her business suit was pale yellow with a straight skirt, stopping just above her knees. It, too, said *no nonsense*. It also said *very feminine*.

"I didn't expect you, Daniel. Did we—"

"No." He shook his head. "I just took a chance and dropped by. I was curious about where you worked. I was wondering what Solutions was. Your card doesn't say."

Monica motioned him into her office. It was an enormous, triangular-shaped room with windows on the two longer sides and a spectacular view of the sage-and-bitter-brush-covered foothills and the pine-topped mountains beyond.

Daniel let out a low whistle as he walked into the center of the room. "Holy cow," he said softly, then turned to face her. "You're president of this company?"

She raised an eyebrow. "As a matter of fact, I own it." The corners of her mouth curved up in a droll smile. "And I think I should be insulted by your tone, Mr. Rourke."

"No. I'm sorry. I didn't mean to be insulting. It's just...I don't know. I didn't expect..." He let his voice trail away, knowing he was going to make it worse if he kept talking.

"You thought all I wanted to do was stay home and be a mommy." She breezed past him and went to stand behind her massive glass-top desk.

He couldn't tell if she was being sarcastic or not. "Sorry," he repeated, just in case.

Monica's gaze swept over the office. When it settled once again on Daniel, she said, "This sort of all just happened. It wasn't what I set out to do."

"I doubt that. About it just happening, I mean. You must have worked hard. I'm impressed. Very impressed."

She shrugged off his words, but he could tell she was pleased.

Daniel again wondered about men in her life. Were there others out there who complimented her on her achievements? Was there anyone serious in her life? She was so beautiful. There must have been plenty of men who had wanted to marry someone like her.

Why haven't you married, Monica?

Before he could ask that question aloud, the door opened behind him. "Monica, dear. Are you ready to—"

He turned toward the familiar voice from his past. "Hello, Mrs. Fletcher."

She paled. "Daniel?"

He knew immediately that Ellen Fletcher hadn't known Monica went to see him at his book signing. And in that instant of strained silence, he recalled the last time he'd spoken to this woman on the phone. "Just leave Monica alone," Ellen had said. "She doesn't want you in her life anymore. Haven't you hurt her enough?"

Monica would have been about five months pregnant with Heather by that time. Ellen Fletcher had to have known he was the father. She could have told him, but she'd chosen not to.

Bitterness burned his throat. He thought he'd gotten past that particular emotion. It looked as though he was wrong.

"I...I didn't expect to see you," Ellen said as she clutched and unclutched the strap on her handbag. Her eyes flicked toward her daughter. "I didn't know anyone was with you, dear. I was early, and Terri wasn't at her desk. I...I'll leave the two of you—"

"It's all right, Mom," Monica replied, sounding calm and unconcerned. "Daniel just dropped by to see the office. You remember he came to Boise to sign his book. Well, he's decided to stay for a while."

"Stay? In Boise?"

He wondered if Ellen was going to faint. He almost took a step toward her, just in case he needed to catch her, then stopped himself from doing so.

"Mother and I have lunch together every Monday at one o'clock."

Daniel turned toward Monica again. She wasn't nearly as calm as she sounded. He could see the tension in her eyes. Despite himself, he felt sorry for her. She obviously had some explaining to do to her mother.

"Listen," he said, "I'll be on my way, let you two get to your lunch."

"Thank you, Daniel." Monica's smile was fleeting.

"I'll call you."

She nodded.

He turned to leave. "Good to see you again, Mrs. Fletcher."

With that lie lingering in the air, he strode out of the office, still not knowing what Solutions was—and not caring, either.

"Good Lord!" Ellen exclaimed the moment the door swung closed behind Daniel. "What on earth—"

"Sit down, Mom." Monica sank onto the chair behind her desk.

Her mother moved forward. "Does he know?"

"Yes."

"Oh, dear heaven." She sat opposite Monica.

"I went to the bookstore on Saturday and told him. He came to the house yesterday to meet Heather." She remembered the way Heather had acted around Daniel. "The two of them got along very well."

"Oh, dear. Oh, dear."

"He's her father. He had a right to know."

There were tears in Ellen's eyes. "He hurt you. He left you. You needed to protect yourself."

Weariness settled heavily on Monica's shoulders. "That was a long time ago, Mom. We were young and foolish. Things are different now."

"Have you told Heather?"

"Not yet. But we will. Soon."

Ellen dabbed at her eyes with a tissue. When she had control of herself once again, she met Monica's gaze and said, "He seemed angry."

"Don't you think he's got a right to be angry? I robbed him out of almost eleven years of Heather's life."

"But what if he hurts her like he did you?"

She paused for a moment, scenes from last evening replaying in her mind. A soothing warmth spread through her, bringing with it a real calm and a sense of peace. "He won't hurt Heather, Mom. He's changed."

She knew without question that she spoke the truth. Daniel would be careful when it came to Heather. He might be ambitious. He might even be ruthless in his role as a big city newspaper reporter. But she would bet money he wouldn't hurt her daughter.

She didn't know why she was so certain of that. She had no reason to be, no basis for her belief. Still, she believed it.

Odd, she had loved the young man she'd known all those years ago. But when she looked at Daniel now, she saw very little of that college boy left. Oh, the outside was much the same, but the inner man was different. And it was the inner Daniel who intrigued Monica. Crazy as it was, she wanted very much to know the man he'd become.

"Monica?"

She gave her head a quick shake, then met her mother's watchful gaze.

"This is all my fault, isn't it?" Ellen glanced down at her folded hands.

"Your fault?"

"Because I never told you that you were adopted."

She chose to answer honestly. "Maybe that was the catalyst, Mom. I won't pretend I wasn't hurt and confused when I found out."

She'd been more than hurt and confused. She'd been stunned. She and her parents had all donated blood while Heather was having her emergency appendectomy. Afterward, the lab technician had made an innocent comment about adoption being a wonderful thing. Monica thought she meant Heather and had corrected her. But the technician had meant Monica and had told her that her blood type didn't match either of her parents; therefore, she had to be adopted.

The discovery had left Monica reeling.

She took a deep breath and continued, "Mom, I know you acted out of love for me...and maybe out of fear, too. I've come to realize the nature of my birth, why I was given up for adoption and who my birth parents were, isn't as important to mc as it is to some. You and Dad are my parents, and I love you." She looked out the windows at the mountains. "But what I did to Daniel wasn't the same thing. I should have told him about Heather from the start. Even if he didn't want to marry me, it was what I should have done. I had no right to keep this a secret from him."

"Monica... You don't still *care* for Daniel, do you?" The question was asked in a tense whisper.

She didn't know what to say. A week ago she could have answered with assurance. Now she didn't know what she felt. Seeing Daniel again after all these years had confused her, left her equilibrium spinning. The best she could do was shrug, nod, then shake her head slowly, a gesture as confused as her emotions.

"I never should have interfered," Ellen said, more to

herself than to her daughter. Her complexion seemed somewhat grayish.

Monica reached for her purse, suddenly more concerned for her mother than for herself. "Come on." She stood. "Let's go have our lunch. This will all sort itself out, Mom. You'll see. It'll be okay."

Daniel pulled the rental car over to the curb in front of the small, white house on Eighth Street. Remnants of anger made his chest tight, but who he was the most angry with he couldn't decide.

He got out of the car and walked around to the sidewalk. There, he paused and stared at the house. Huge, ancient maples and oaks, their trunks gnarled and misshapen, stretched their leafy branches over the house and yard. The sidewalk was rippled and cracked by tree roots butting up against its underside. Grass grew sparsely, like a balding man's hair, because the trees obscured the sunlight.

This had been Monica's dream house. She'd found it quite by accident, the year they were both sophomores at Boise State. Countless times after that, they had walked past it, strolling hand in hand in the cool of an evening. Monica had always stopped and looked at it and then talked about how fun it would be to live in an "adorable" little house like that, children playing in the fenced backyard.

It had scared him to death.

He'd wanted so much more than domesticity. He'd wanted more than what Boise could offer him.

And he'd found it, too. He'd lived an exciting life since graduating and moving away. He had a spacious corner apartment in an exclusive high-rise building on the northside of Chicago with views of both Lake Mich-

igan and the city. He had a job where he was respected.
He made more money than he'd ever expected to be
making at the age of thirty-three. One might even say
he was famous. Shoot, even young receptionists in
Boise, Idaho, knew who Daniel Rourke was. At least by
name.

He stared at the little white house with its peeling
paint on the eaves, its uneven, patchy lawn and its
cracked sidewalks, and he wondered why fame and fortune didn't seem to be enough anymore, why he felt
strangely empty.

Monica had done well, too. Yet he had a sneaky feeling her happiness didn't have much to do with her nice
office on the ninth floor of a ritzy office complex or her
attractive home in an upscale neighborhood. He suspected she would have been just as happy living in this
small house in the north end.

For some reason, it irritated him, knowing she was
content while he was still searching.

Daniel yanked his cell phone out of his hip pocket
and flipped it open. He jabbed the fluorescent green
numbers, then pressed Send and listened to the ensuing
ring.

"Good afternoon. Solutions."

He recognized the voice of the receptionist. "This is
Daniel Rourke. I need to speak to Monica."

"I'm sorry, Mr. Rourke. Ms. Fletcher hasn't returned
from lunch with her mother. May I give her a—"

"Tell her to call me." He recited his number.

The receptionist repeated it, then said, "I'll give her
the message."

"Thanks." He flipped the phone closed.

Monica had a raging headache by the time she returned to the office. It didn't improve when she saw the

name and phone number on the message slip.

Monica... You don't still care for Daniel, do you?

"Of course not," she muttered as she lifted the receiver and dialed. "But he *is* Heather's father."

He answered on the third ring. "Hello?"

"Daniel, it's Monica. You left a message to call?"

"Yeah, I was hoping I could take Heather on a picnic this weekend. Maybe go up to the hot springs in Idaho City."

Her pulse quickened, along with her anxiety level. "Just the two of you?"

Silence. Then, "No, I don't suppose that would be a good idea. She'd wonder why. I'm still somewhat of a stranger to her. It probably isn't time to tell her the truth yet."

Her headache worsened. She massaged her right temple with her index and middle fingers. "Not yet," she said in a strained voice.

She was afraid, and it had a lot to do with her mother. At lunch, Ellen had asked if Monica wasn't worried he might try to get custody. The thought hadn't occurred to her before. But now...

"Okay, how about I pick you both up on Saturday at ten in the morning? Does that work for you?"

She tightened her grip on the receiver. She had set her course, now she had to see it through. "Yes. We'll be ready."

He didn't say anything for a moment. The silence seemed deafening. She wondered what he was thinking, what he wanted to say to her. Years ago, she would have known what to expect. But Daniel wasn't the same man any more than she was the same woman. Years of experiences, disappointments, successes, and day-to-day life had changed them both. Now she didn't have any idea what was running through his head.

She wished she did.

"I'll bring the food and drinks," he finally said, still giving her no clue to his thoughts, "if you'll bring the plates and utensils."

"Okay."

"Don't forget your swimming suits."

"We won't."

"See you Saturday."

She waited until the other end of the line went dead, then placed the receiver in its cradle.

For a moment, she simply stared at the phone, watching as the lights for the various lines flickered on and off as others in the office conducted their business. Then she turned and walked to the large window facing the mountains. She stared upward, toward Schaefer Butte, the wheels in her head churning.

What had she to fear? Daniel was only here for a few months. That's what he had told her on Saturday. Just until September. He wasn't going to make a drastic change in his life—and having a daughter living with him would certainly be a drastic change. If he didn't know that now, she would make certain he'd know it before he left Boise.

No, Daniel would go back to his life in Chicago at the end of summer, and Monica's life would return to normal.

Well, almost normal.

Daniel did *seem* truly interested in Heather. He would probably write to her or call her on the telephone. Maybe he would come to Boise to see Heather on occasion. He might even want her to visit him in Chicago for a week or two every summer. That's the way divorced parents handled such things. She and Daniel could make it work for Heather, too.

She thought of Ellen again, of the strained expression on her face, of the way she'd said, ''I never should have interfered.''

Monica hadn't given those words much thought at the time, but suddenly she realized it had been an odd thing for her mother to say. She couldn't recall a time when Ellen had interfered with Monica's relationship with Daniel. Even after he'd moved out and the engagement had been broken, Ellen had never said a negative word about him. She'd kept her thoughts private when Monica announced she was pregnant. In fact, her mother had been a rock, completely supportive.

In what way, she wondered, did Ellen think she'd interfered?

Chapter Four

Monica was awake before six on Saturday morning, her nerves screeching. She told herself she was being ridiculous, she had no cause to be nervous, but it didn't help. She'd done nothing but think about Daniel all week long. Her thoughts had thrust her backward in time, and she'd relived many moments—*too* many moments— when they had been together. She'd remembered both the good and the not so good times.

But it was the memory of their lovemaking that had left her tense and edgy. She didn't want to remember the way he used to make her feel. It was old news. Finished. It was most definitely unwelcome.

As for Heather, she was delighted to be going up to the hot springs. It sure beat what was too often their Saturday morning routine of housecleaning and other chores. And she seemed equally delighted to be seeing Daniel again.

That was a good thing, Monica reminded herself as she placed plastic plates and other picnic ware into a wicker basket on the kitchen counter. If Daniel was going to be a permanent part of Heather's life, it was important her daughter—*their* daughter—be fond of him.

She cast an anxious glance at the clock on the wall. Nine forty-five. He would be here soon.

She stepped from the kitchen into the hallway. "Heather," she called up the stairs. "Are you ready?"

"I'm looking for my nose plugs. Have you seen them?"

"Not since last summer."

Heather appeared at the top of the stairs. "Well, I can't go swimming without them," she said, a panicked look in her eyes, her voice rising. "Getting water up my nose makes me sick. You know that!"

"Did you check the bottom drawer in your bathroom?"

"No." Her face brightened instantly. Then she disappeared into her bathroom. A moment later, she hollered, "They're here. I found 'em."

Another crisis averted in the life of a ten-year-old. Monica couldn't help but smile.

The doorbell rang, and her smile vanished.

Help me get through this day, she prayed silently, then walked to the door and opened it.

If Daniel had been a male model, he could have sold a gazillion pairs of faded jeans, the way he looked in them. He wore a dark teal T-shirt that nicely revealed the form of his chest muscles and biceps. His short black hair was stylishly spiky. His smile was straight out of Hollywood—white teeth in a handsome, tanned face.

"Hi," he said. "You two ready?"

Monica couldn't remember the last time she'd been left breathless at the sight of a man.

His brows drew together in a slight frown. "I'm not too early, am I?"

Get a grip! she silently commanded herself as she opened the door wider, offering a quick smile. "Of course not. Come in. I'll get our things." She turned her back to him and called, "Heather? Mr. Rourke is here. Let's go."

Monica hurried to the kitchen, still mentally scolding herself. What was the matter? This wasn't at all like her. She had long ago learned to ignore any feelings of attraction toward the opposite sex. There'd been no room in her life for a man. She'd had a daughter to raise and a business to run.

And, she added as she leaned against the kitchen counter and closed her eyes, she hadn't wanted to risk her heart again after Daniel.

"Need help?"

She jumped and gasped at the sound of his voice. She spun around.

"Sorry." But he didn't look the least bit sorry. "Didn't mean to scare you."

"You didn't *scare* me." She sounded waspish but she was unable to help it. She *felt* waspish.

He stepped into the kitchen. His voice lowered. "Have I done something to upset you, Monica?" His gray eyes looked deep into hers.

Her mouth was dry. Her throat ached. She shook her head but knew the response was a lie. He *had* done something to upset her. He'd made her feel things she didn't want to feel, and she resented him for doing so.

Still meeting her gaze, he reached out with his right hand for the picnic basket. Then with his left hand, he took hold of her right arm at the elbow. "Come on. Let's have a good day, the three of us." His voice lowered another notch. "We can make this work, Monica, if we just try."

She nodded, her heart thumping, her skin warm beneath his fingers.

"I'm ready, Mama!" Heather called from the front door.

Her daughter's voice served to rein in Monica's careening emotions. She forced a smile. "Yes, let's go." She gently pulled free of Daniel's grasp and led the way out of the house.

The highway climbed its way through the foothills and into the mountains. With the convertible's top down, Daniel drove at a comfortable speed for the winding road, enjoying the scenery.

Fifteen minutes into the drive, Heather spotted a fox dashing up a hillside. Not long after, they passed a doe and her fawn grazing on a plateau on the far side of a deep ravine. The air was sweetened by the scent of pine trees. The stream running parallel to the road churned and gurgled and bumped over smooth stones, the water high with spring runoff.

Daniel was surprised by the strong sense of rightness that tightened his chest. He hadn't known he'd missed all this. Extending his sabbatical had been a good thing. He would be able to relax, find out what he needed to do next with his life, do some prioritizing.

Get to know his daughter.

"Look!" Heather exclaimed from the back seat.

After a quick glance over his shoulder, he followed the direction of her outstretched arm and spied the eagle soaring overhead. "That's something you don't see in

Chicago,'' he commented, more to himself than to anyone else.

''I suppose not,'' Monica replied.

It was the first time she'd spoken since they'd left her home. He'd blamed part of that on the open car, the wind in their ears and all. Of course, it hadn't stopped Heather from talking. She'd filled him in on her best friend's new mare and how Heather hoped to have a horse of her own one day and the book she'd just read and some of the plans she had for this summer, including two weeks at Girl Scout camp in August.

Daniel hadn't known kids talked this much. But then, what did he know about kids? He'd rarely been around them.

He glanced sideways at Monica. She used to talk about wanting three kids. From what he'd seen, she was a good mom. A pity she'd never married and had a brother or a sister for Heather.

The image of Monica with another man didn't set well with him, but he chose not to analyze why.

It wasn't too late for her to have more kids. She was only thirty-three. Plenty of women—even career women—were having babies in their thirties. But maybe Monica didn't want more children now. Maybe she'd found out one was enough.

He cast another quick glance in her direction. The wind whipped her blond ponytail against the back of her head and neck in a merry mix-up fashion. She didn't look like a mom and career woman. Right now she looked like a teenager with her whole life still ahead of her.

He wondered what she'd want to do with her life if she could start over. Then he wondered if she would want *him* if she had it to do over.

Almost as if she'd heard his thoughts, she turned her head and met his gaze. Her hair slapped her cheek, and she held it back with her right hand.

She was so darned beautiful.

He looked back at the road, his hands tightening on the wheel. He felt as if the car was spinning out of control. Only it wasn't the car. It was his thoughts that were out of control. Totally out of control.

The day was just cool enough to make swimming in the hot springs enjoyable. The warm water didn't slow Heather down one bit, but it made Monica lethargic. It soothed the rough edges of her emotions.

Lying crosswise on an air mattress, her chin resting on the back of her hands, she lazily moved her feet while watching Daniel boost Heather with his cupped hands, sending her flying up out of the water into the air. Heather squealed before splashing down into the water again. Daniel grinned the entire time.

He looked as good all wet as he had in his T-shirt and jeans. Maybe better. Water glistened on his chest, a tanned, well-defined chest with just enough dark hair to be sexy.

That long dormant feeling of desire stirred again. This time she didn't resist it. She let it spread through her unchecked. She could imagine him kissing her, caressing her, stroking her. For just a moment, it was almost as if he were making love to her in the swimming pool. Her nipples puckered. She ached with wanting.

She closed her eyes and savored the sensations.

Then she heard Heather squeal in delight again, and Monica remembered why she was there. For Heather. For Heather and Daniel, daughter and father. Not for herself.

She looked at them again, saw Daniel dunk down in the water, preparing to lift Heather for the countless time. He had great patience, she realized. It was something he'd acquired while he was away from Boise. The Daniel she'd known before had been a very impatient sort. She wondered what else about him had changed.

Heather resurfaced after being airborne. This time, instead of swimming back to Daniel, she headed toward Monica. "Hey, Mama, you wanna try it? I bet Mr. Rourke's strong enough to toss you, too."

She thought of his biccps, flexed as he propelled Heather upward. Yes, he probably could toss her quite easily. She felt as if he already had.

Suddenly Daniel was there beside her, grinning and golden bronzed and glistening with water droplets. "I'm hungry. Shall we eat?"

She nodded, glad he wasn't offering to do as Heather had suggested.

Half an hour later—all of them changed into dry clothes but with their hair still damp—they spread a blanket in the shade of a tree and set out their picnic things. Daniel had filled a cooler with foods from a deli. There was fried chicken, sliced sandwich meats, two kinds of bread and four salads. He'd chosen several different sodas, not knowing what anyone else liked, and had also brought bottled water, just in case. Monica didn't even want to think about the yummy looking desserts she'd spied in the cooler.

The swim had made them all hungry. Conversation was kept to a minimum while they ate. Even Heather was quiet for a short time. But then she saw a friend from school and asked if she could go play.

"As long as you don't run off out of sight," Monica answered.

She watched as Heather dashed down the hillside.

And then she was alone with Daniel. She turned her head slowly. He was watching her with those intent gray eyes of his.

"Why *did* you tell me about her?" he asked gently. "She's happy, well-adjusted. She doesn't seem to need me in her life. Why, after all these years?"

"Because it was the right thing to do."

He leaned slightly forward. "*Why,* Monica?"

There was something in his gaze that told her he wasn't going to let her off easily this time. He wanted the truth. All of it. The way he watched her must have been the same way he looked at people he was investigating for a story, the sort of look that demanded honesty, whether a person wanted to be honest or not. It was impossible to turn away from him. His gaze seemed to hold her, refusing to let go.

In a whisper, she replied, "Last month I found out I was adopted as a baby."

He raised an eyebrow. Nothing more. Nothing that would reveal what her news made him think or feel.

"Mom and Dad kept it a secret from me all my life. When I found out, I...I felt betrayed."

He remained silent, but she sensed his empathy.

She swallowed the unexpected lump in her throat and continued, "It made me realize that what I had done to you was just as bad. Worse actually."

"Why worse?"

"Mom and Dad thought they were protecting me from feeling abandoned." She drew a deep breath. "But I think I must have wanted to punish you for leaving me. I didn't realize it at the time, but that doesn't make it any less true."

He nodded slowly, as if digesting what she'd said.

After a long while, he asked, "Have you tried to find out anything about your birth parents?"

She frowned as she dropped her gaze to her clasped hands. She hadn't expected her revelation to take the conversation in this direction. "No."

"Do you want to? Find out who your birth parents are?"

"I don't think so."

"It's much easier to get that information these days. I did a story on it once." There was a lengthy pause, then he added, "I'd bc glad to help you while I'm here."

Her mind focused on his last words rather than his first. *While I'm here.* His stay in Boise was temporary. It was important she remember that.

She met his gaze. "Daniel, what about Heather?"

Again he raised an eyebrow but said nothing.

"What I mean is, do you plan to see her once you go back to Chicago? Once she knows you're her father..." She let her voice trail into silence.

He looked down the hillside to whcre Heather was playing a game of tag with her friend and some other children. His black brows drew together and his eycs narrowed. He ran his right thumb along his jawline, a gesture she had already learned meant he was deep in thought.

At long last, he looked at Monica again. "Yes." It was a firm, simple, no argument kind of answer.

She saw a flicker of something in the depths of his mercurial gray eyes, something poignant but indefinable. Her pulse quickened, along with her breathing. When he glanced away, she was both relieved and disappointed.

"Whcn in September is her birthday?" he asked, his voice low, his gaze locked on Heather again.

"The fifteenth."

"How much did she weigh when she was born?"

"Seven pounds four ounces."

"Did she have lots of hair?"

"Yes. Black, just like it is now."

"Was she a pretty baby?"

His words caused tears to well up in her eyes and her throat to constrict, making it difficult to reply. "The prettiest I've ever seen." She swallowed hard. "I have photos if you'd like to see them."

"Yes," he answered softly. "I would."

Silence stretched between them for several minutes. Then Daniel spoke again. "Was she born at St. Luke's or St. Al's?"

"Neither. She was born in Salt Lake City."

He turned toward her, clearly surprised. "Why Salt Lake?"

How little we know about each other? she thought, sadness piercing her heart.

"Why Salt Lake?" he asked again.

"Because you were still at Boise State for most of my pregnancy. I didn't want to chance running into you before you graduated and moved away." She pulled her knees up to her chest and clasped her arms around them, then rested her forehead against her knees. "Because I went there intending to give the baby up for adoption."

A memory rushed in, replacing the present. She was in her girlhood bedroom, leaning over a suitcase, packing to leave for Salt Lake City. Her mother was standing in the doorway behind her.

"You're doing the right thing," Ellen had said. "There's a loving couple out there somewhere who can't have children of their own. They're waiting for a child only you can give them. You're doing the best thing for this baby, dear. As hard as it is now, you're doing what's right.''

Suddenly her mother's words took on new meaning. Ellen had been talking about herself, about her own inability to have children. It seemed so clear to Monica now. She wondered why she hadn't guessed the truth back then.

Daniel's words intruded on her thoughts. ''Why didn't you, Monica?''

She lifted her head to look at him. ''Why didn't I what?''

''Why didn't you give Heather up for adoption? You must have known how difficult it would be, raising her alone. You were young. Unmarried.''

Monica smiled as more memories flooded her. ''You don't know how really hard it will be until you're doing it. Two o'clock feedings. Colic. Doctor bills. Walking the floor for hours. Never enough sleep. Formula and diapers and child care. But the moment I saw her, I knew I couldn't give her away.''

She looked like you even then. The thought brought with it a sharp longing, and her tears returned.

''I'm sorry, Monica.''

She closed her eyes, shook her head.

''If I'd known…''

Silence returned, for there was no perfect ending to Daniel's unfinished sentence. The past could not be undone, and both of them knew it.

Heather's laughter drew Daniel's gaze away from Monica and down the hillside. The sound touched a deep and empty corner of his heart. Strange. He hadn't known the corner was empty until he'd met Heather.

''Monica, it's time to tell her who I am.''

He heard her tiny intake of breath, but he didn't look toward her.

"You know I'm right. We can't go on pretending I'm just Mr. Rourke, an old college buddy. She should know who I am."

She touched his arm, drawing his gaze first to her fingertips, then to her face. "Once we tell her, your life will never be the same."

"It won't ever be the same anyway." He spoke more sharply than he'd intended.

She drew back as if scalded. Her face paled and her eyes rounded.

"Sorry," he muttered. He drew a deep breath, then gently repeated, "I'm sorry, Monica. I didn't mean for that to sound like it did. I know you're concerned about what my role will be with Heather. I'm not totally blind. I'm not going to hurt her. I swear it."

Softly she said, "She's going to want to love you, Daniel. She's going to want you to be a real father to her and to love her in return. She's also going to be hurt and confused. She might resent me for not telling her before now, for not telling you. I know it isn't going to be easy for any of us at first." She paused a long time before asking, "Will you be around long enough for us to work it through?"

He didn't care for the accusation behind her question, but he was honest enough to admit she had a right to ask it. Beyond work, he'd never committed himself to much of anything. He was a great one for saying, *We'll see.* What a cop-out!

He couldn't cop out now with those same words. She was asking him to make a commitment to Heather, a commitment he'd never been able to make to Monica herself. Heck, he'd never made that kind of commitment to another human being.

But somehow the words came out. "I'll be around. Whatever it takes, I'll be here."

And he meant it, he realized, with no small amount of surprise.

Daniel could feel Monica's tension during the drive back to Boise. He tried to take her mind off of what was awaiting them when they reached her home by asking about her business. Although she answered, he didn't think he'd succeeded in lessening her anxiety.

"Solutions is a secretarial and bookkeeping service. We have staff accountants and provide computerized bookkeeping off-site for those who want it. And we have a branch that serves as a temp agency." It was obvious she spoke by rote and that her thoughts remained elsewhere.

Daniel persevered. "Are you the sole owner or do you have a partner?"

"No, it's just me." She glanced over at him. "I started it from scratch."

He let out a low whistle. "Impressive. Tell me about it. Tell me how it came to be what it is today."

From the look she gave him, she understood exactly what he was doing. She even managed a tight smile. "It wasn't because of any grand plan, that's for certain. I just wanted to be at home with Heather as much as possible, so I started out by freelance bookkeeping and maintaining large mailing lists on my computer. Lots of small businesses still weren't computerized back then so I found my services in demand. Later, I helped a lot of those same companies buy their own computers and trained their personnel to use them. I diversified, hired some employees. Somehow it ballooned from there.''

Daniel glanced over his shoulder, intending to ask Heather what she thought about her mom's business, but he discovered she was asleep. Her legs were drawn up on the seat, and her head was resting against the window of the right rear door.

Monica laughed softly. ''I guess the warm water wore her out.''

''Yeah.'' He stared at the road ahead. ''I guess so.'' Unexpectedly he found he was now the nervous one. What if he turned out to be a terrible father? What if just telling her the truth screwed her up no end? How would he fix that?

As if understanding his inner turmoil, Monica took her turn at asking a question. ''Was the trial as bad as it seemed on television?''

It took him a moment to even realize what she was talking about. When he did, he answered, ''Yeah, it was bad. You spend all those months, looking at the face of evil, it begins to haunt you in your sleep.''

''But now there's your book about the case. You're famous, Daniel. That must be rewarding.''

Rewarding? He wasn't sure if that was the right word for it. Mostly he was relieved it was over. He wanted to put it all behind him.

''It's what you wanted,'' Monica added. ''Back in college. To be famous.''

Fame isn't all it's cracked up to be, he almost said to her. But how could he? That's why he'd left her. Left her alone and pregnant, as it had turned out. So how did he tell her he'd been mistaken, that he'd been chasing the wrong dream for the past decade? How did he tell her he wasn't satisfied with what he'd accomplished, that it wasn't enough, that there was still something missing?

Not that it had all been bad. Daniel had always found working for the newspaper an exciting challenge. He liked writing about people, *real* people. He liked finding clues and being the one to figure things out. He liked being the first to break a story. He'd put in long hours through the years, walked a lot of beats, worked his way up through the ranks to become a respected journalist.

But he'd missed being home in Boise. Funny how that worked. He hadn't known he'd missed it until he was back. Now that he was here, it seemed as clear as glass.

He wondered what else he would discover, if he stayed here long enough.

Maybe he'd find out Heather didn't want him to be her dad. Maybe he'd find out he couldn't be here for her as he'd sworn only a short time ago.

He gave his head a quick shake to clear it. Then he glanced over at Monica. "I think we ought to wait to have this talk with Heather. Let's give it another week."

Even though he was again watching the road, he knew she looked at him, knew there was disappointment in her eyes. "Sure, Daniel. Whatever you think."

He felt as if he'd just walked out on her—and Heather—a second time.

Chapter Five

It was the persistent ringing of the doorbell that awakened Daniel at nine-thirty in the morning after a night of troubled slumber.

Disheveled and feeling out of sorts, he went to answer the door. He didn't bother to grab his robe on the way out of his bedroom. He fully intended to send the intruder on his way, then go straight back to bed.

The man on the other side of the screen door grinned at him. "Well, I'll be damned. It *is* you. Mom said she saw you driving down the street, but I didn't believe her."

Daniel blinked, glowered, ran a hand through his hair. "Do I know you?"

The fellow's grin broadened. "Don't recognize me, huh? Take a good look, Danny boy."

If this was some publicity seeker…

"Maybe if I was wearing a pair of dweeb eyeglasses and weighed about sixty pounds more?"

Daniel pushed open the screen door. "Tony?"

He couldn't believe it. He'd known Tony Cristobal since the second grade. They'd grown up together in this neighborhood, had ridden their bikes up and down this very same street. The last time he'd seen his boyhood friend, Tony had been wearing eyeglasses with soda bottle lenses and had weighed in at a hefty two hundred and fifty pounds.

"In the flesh. But there's a lot less flesh now."

Wide-awake, Daniel slapped Tony on the back. "How the heck are you? Come on in."

"I'm good. Real good." Tony stepped into the house. He cast an amused glance at Daniel's pajama bottoms and bare feet. "So this is how the rich and famous live? Hmm."

"Yeah. We just lie around all day, drinking coffee and watching TV." He motioned for Tony to follow him. "And speaking of coffee, I need some." He led the way into the kitchen.

While Daniel filled the coffeepot's reservoir with cold water, Tony pulled out a chair and sat down at the table. "Your dad's place hasn't changed much."

"Not much." He measured grounds into the filter. When he was finished, he flipped the switch on, then turned toward the table and leaned against the counter while crossing his arms over his chest. "So tell me what's up. It's been a long time since we saw each other."

"Thirteen years in June."

Daniel remembered. It had been at Tony's and Jennifer's wedding. Daniel had served as Tony's best man. The bride had been four months pregnant. With a new wife and a baby on the way, Tony hadn't been able to afford to continue in college. The newlyweds had left for California right after the wedding. Tony had had a construction job waiting for him there, working for one of his numerous uncles. Daniel had kept in touch with his friend for a few years, but eventually, the calls and correspondence had dried up.

"So when did you come back to Boise, Tony? Are you living here now?"

"Yeah. Moved back a few years ago." He tilted his chair onto its back legs. "I wanted to be close to the folks. My mom hasn't been too well."

"Sorry to hear it. I hope it's not serious."

"No. Not yet. But we didn't want to wait until it was."

"And what about Jennifer? How's she?" He wasn't sure he should ask. For all he knew, the two were divorced by this time. "And your little boy? What was his name?"

"Mikolas. And everybody's fine. Jennifer and I bought a big old farmhouse on a couple of acres out near Star. We needed lots of room. There's eight of us now."

Daniel felt his eyes widen and his jaw go slack.

Tony laughed. "Yup. I've got six kids. Catalin is the youngest and the only girl. She just turned one this winter. And from what I've seen, she's going to be spoiled rotten by her brothers."

"Tony, the family man." Daniel was unable to disguise the surprise in his voice. "Six kids."

"Guess that sounds pretty strange to a high-living bachelor like you. But I gotta say, being a husband and a dad is the absolute best. I wouldn't trade my wife or a single one of my kids for anything."

Daniel thought of Monica and Heather.

"'Course," Tony continued, seemingly oblivious to the direction of Daniel's thoughts, "I guess if my dad had been married as often as yours, I might've been wary of matrimony, too. I wasn't surprised when I heard you and Monica split up, but I sure thought you were an idiot for letting her get away."

Daniel pictured Monica in her red, one-piece swim suit, her golden hair caught high in a ponytail. *An idiot for letting her get away...* He wondered—

"Have you seen her since you got back? She's done mighty well for herself. Got her own business. She and Jennifer talk on the phone occasionally, but we don't get to see much of her. Our lives are too hectic." The tone of his voice altered slightly. "She's got a little girl of her own. Heather. A real sweetheart."

The coffeepot quit gurgling, and Daniel was glad for an excuse to turn away from his old friend. Something told him Tony had guessed Heather was his daughter. Given the striking physical resemblance and when she was born, he supposed he'd have had to be blind—even stupid—not to guess. Still, Daniel wasn't ready to talk about it, so he changed the subject.

"Did you go back to college to finish your degree?" he asked.

"Nope. Couldn't afford to, not with a growing family like mine."

Daniel looked over his shoulder, holding up a mug in question.

"Sure," Tony answered. "I'll take a cup. Black."

He poured a second mugful of coffee and carried both to the table. He handed Tony his, then sat down in the chair opposite him.

"I'm still doing construction," his friend continued.

"It's had its ups and downs over the years, but we get by. Keeps the kids in sneakers."

"Ever sorry? About giving up college, I mean. You really would have been a great architect. It was like an art with you. I remember all those buildings you used to design in your basement. You could have made quite a name for yourself."

Tony looked thoughtful for a moment, his gaze locked on his coffee mug. "What you really mean is, did I resent Jennifer for getting pregnant? The answer is, no." He met Daniel's gaze. "I loved her, man. Still do. Making a name for myself was never as important to me as it was you. I wasn't ever that ambitious. I just want to do right by my family. That's what's most important to me."

Again Daniel thought of Monica and Heather. It was tempting to tell Tony that he'd met his daughter. But what right had he to do so?

None.

At least, not yet.

Members of the congregation stood outside the church, visiting with one another after Sunday services. Monica was glad she'd worn a sweater. Last night's rainstorm had dropped the temperature about fifteen degrees.

Heather didn't seem to mind the cooler weather. Her laughter rang in the spring air as she ran with some friends in the park that bordered the small nondenominational church the Fletchers attended. Watching her daughter, Monica's heart ached. She wished there was someone she could talk to about her confused feelings.

She'd been disappointed by Daniel's decision to wait to tell Heather he was her father. And yet, she'd also been terrified when he'd said it was time to tell her, wondering if it wasn't too soon.

Even the reasons for her disappointment were confused. Partly it was because Daniel wasn't sure he was ready to be a father just yet. She even respected him for being cautious, for not wanting to risk hurting Heather. But part of the reason for her disappointment was that she'd felt Daniel pulling away from her.

This isn't about me, she reminded herself for what seemed to be the hundredth time since yesterday afternoon.

What horrified her was the part of her that wished it *was* about her. She kept envisioning Daniel in his swimming trunks, his body tanned and toned, his skin glistening with water beads, grinning as he hoisted Heather into the air. Monica was overwhelmed at the most inappropriate moments with a longing to feel his arms around her, to see if his kisses still sent her spinning and reeling.

"Is it true, Monica?"

She felt her face flush, as if she'd been caught in Daniel's arms instead of just daydreaming about it. Fighting for composure, she turned toward her mother. "Is what true?" she asked as innocently as possible.

"Heather told me you spent yesterday with Daniel."

She suppressed a sigh. "Yes, Mother, it's true."

"Do you think that's wise?"

"We've been over this already."

"But—"

"Mom, you've got to let me handle this the way I think is best."

Ellen obviously wanted to say more, but she restrained herself.

Monica offered a conciliatory smile. "It's going to be

okay. Daniel and I didn't make it as a couple, but it doesn't mean we can't be good parents.''

''I just don't want you or Heather to get hurt. I can't help remembering how devastated you were when—''

''You can't protect us from life, Mom.'' Monica put her arm around her mother's shoulders and gave her a squeeze.

Ellen Fletcher had always been there for her daughter. When Monica had announced she was pregnant with Daniel's baby, Ellen hadn't placed blame or made Monica feel guilty for her mistakes. She had done everything to make those difficult months easier. Ellen had gone with Monica to Salt Lake City and helped her get settled into an apartment where she'd awaited the birth of the baby. Her mother had been supportive of her plans to give the baby up for adoption, but when Monica changed her mind and decided to keep Heather, she hadn't chastised her or tried to talk her out of it.

Monica felt a sudden rush of love for the only mother she'd ever known. Perhaps Ellen and Wayne had been wrong not to tell Monica she was an adopted child, but it didn't lessen the wonderful, caring atmosphere in which she'd been raised. She didn't know why her birth mother had given her up for adoption. She probably would never know. Maybe she had been a girl much like Monica herself, rejected by the man she'd loved. Maybe she hadn't been lucky enough to have a mother like Ellen Fletcher, a mother who would stand by her, no matter what.

''I love you, Mom,'' she said softly as she met her mother's worried gaze.

Ellen's eyes glistened with tears.

''I'm trying to do the right thing.''

''I know.'' Her mother nodded. ''I know.''

Once again, Monica envisioned Daniel with Heather. Once again, she felt a tightening in her chest, a longing for something still undefined. "Does it ever get easier to know what we should do?" she whispered, a catch in her voice.

"I'm afraid not, dear. You just have to muddle through, one day at a time. Just like the rest of us."

Her mother's words replayed in her head when Monica and Heather arrived home to find Daniel's red convertible parked in front of their house.

"It's Mr. Rourke!" Heather said excitedly. "You think he wants to go back to the hot springs?"

"I doubt it, honey. Not this soon. You probably wore him out yesterday."

As Monica pulled her minivan into the driveway, the convertible's driver-side door opened and Daniel stepped out of the car. Monica felt a little flutter in her chest but strove to ignore it.

She turned the key, cutting the engine. Before she could even reach for the door, Heather had already clamored out her side and was racing toward Daniel.

"Hi, Mr. Rourke. We weren't expectin' to see you today."

Monica got out of the van.

Heather took hold of her father's hand and pulled him toward the driveway. "Doesn't Mama look pretty? That's my favorite dress of hers."

Daniel removed his sunglasses. "Yeah, she looks real pretty."

Flustered, Monica dropped her gaze to a spot on the ground midway between them.

"Prettiest woman I've seen in a long time."

Her heart started an unwelcome clamoring in her

chest. One would think she'd never received a compli-ment before.

"Tony Cristobal came by the house this morning. I didn't even recognize him."

Relieved by the change of subject, she glanced up. "He looks great, doesn't he?"

"I guess keeping up with six kids will do that to a fellow."

"They're quite the lively bunch. I should give Jennifer a call. We haven't managed to get together since last summer."

Daniel's expression grew serious. "He knows, doesn't he?"

She didn't have to ask what he meant. "I think so, but he's never said anything."

"It's time to have that talk."

She swallowed hard, then nodded.

"Mama, can we ask Mr. Rourke to stay for lunch?"

Monica looked at her daughter, feeling afraid and hoping she didn't show it. "Sure, honey."

"Can you, Mr. Rourke? Can you stay and eat with us?"

"Yes," he answered simply. "I'll stay."

How long will you stay, Daniel? Only three more months? Is that all?

An image popped into her head. An image of Daniel holding her close, their bodies pressed tightly together as he kissed her. Her skin tingled. She felt warm all over.

Three months won't be long enough.

Panicked by her thoughts, she turned away, closed the car door and hurried up the walk to the house.

Heather deserved a dad, she reminded herself, and Daniel deserved to know his daughter. That's what this was all about. That was the only thing this was about. A father and a daughter. Not a man and a woman.

She fumbled with the key in the lock.

How long had it been since she'd thought about a man's touch, since she'd pictured herself enjoying a man's kisses? Too long. That's why she was imagining Daniel holding her, kissing her. It was only because she'd emotionally shut herself away from men for so long. *Too* long. It wasn't because of Daniel. It couldn't possibly be because of Daniel.

"I'm going upstairs to change," she called over her shoulder, not looking to see if the other two had followed her up the walk or if they'd heard what she'd said.

In her room, she closed the door, then leaned against it, her eyes closed.

This was insane. It was crazy. There was no reason in the world that she should be thinking such things, feeling such things.

She drew in a ragged breath, then slowly exhaled. Better. That was better. The foolishness had nearly passed. She was almost back in control again.

Almost.

Daniel didn't have time to wonder about Monica's quick retreat up the stairs. Heather took charge of him, leading him into the family room. He sat down in the chair opposite the sofa. Heather sat on the matching ottoman in front of him.

"Guess what I forgot to tell you yesterday, Mr. Rourke?"

"Haven't a clue."

"I won a prize for a story I wrote in school. Mrs. Kline, my teacher, is gonna have me read it on Friday at the school carnival. All the kids who won will be reading their stuff. My best friend Mary won for her poem about horses, but I won for my short story.''

"That's terrific, Heather. What's the prize?''

She shrugged. "It's a secret. I won't know until Friday.'' Her eyes widened. "Gee, do you think you could come with us? To the carnival, I mean.''

Daniel wished Monica would come back. He wasn't sure what he should answer.

"I just thought you might wanna hear my story, you bein' a famous writer and all.''

He was surprised by how good that made him feel, his daughter wanting him to hear her work.

"Please come, Mr. Rourke. Mama'd like you to. I know she would. She thinks you're real nice.''

"Does she?'' He glanced toward the stairs. If only it was as simple as Heather made it sound. Everybody liking everybody. No past to stumble over.

"Sure, she does. I can tell. She's never had a boyfriend like you who comes over a lot.''

Before Daniel could respond, Monica appeared at the bottom of the staircase. She had changed into jeans and a simple white blouse. The long sleeves were rolled up to her elbows. Her feet were bare. How was it she managed to look beautiful, even when dressed so simply?

"Mama, I just invited Mr. Rourke to go to the school carnival on Friday.'' She ran across the room to where her mother was standing. "That's okay, isn't it? You'd like him to come, too, wouldn't you?''

Monica's and Daniel's gazes met and held for an instant. He could feel her tension. The air crackled with it.

Don't hurt Heather, her eyes seemed to say. *Please don't fail her like you failed me.*

Yes, he'd failed her. He'd told her he loved her, but

he'd never wanted to make a real commitment to her or to marriage. Not when he'd thought the whole world was awaiting him elsewhere. So he'd intentionally driven her away from him, one angry word at a time.

And look what that decision had cost him.

Monica looked at Heather. "We need to talk, honey."

"But what about the carnival—"

"Let's talk first. Sit down, please. On the sofa."

A puzzled expression crossed the child's face as she moved to obey. Monica sat beside her daughter, then took hold of Heather's hand, as if afraid the girl might run away.

Daniel's mouth was dry. He wished he could get himself a drink of water—or something stronger.

"Heather, honey," Monica began, her voice soft. "Mr. Rourke and I have something important to tell you."

Heather glanced between the two of them, then grinned that mischievous grin of hers. "Are you getting married? That'd be way cool."

Daniel hadn't seen that one coming. He suspected Monica hadn't, either.

"No," Monica answered without looking in his direction. "No, we are *not* getting married. Where would you get such an idea?"

"I can tell you like him a lot. And he keeps coming over. He's awful nice and you always seem—"

"Heather, please." Monica's tone was sharp. "That's enough."

Daniel got up from his chair and crossed to the sofa. He was moving by instinct now. He didn't know what he was planning to do or say.

Heather turned to look at him as he sat down on her other side. Her smile had vanished. Her mouth quivered, and she looked like she was fighting tears. He suspected her mother rarely raised her voice to scold.

He took hold of her free hand. "Do me a favor, Heather. Just listen to your mom and me for a second, will you?"

She nodded.

"Remember we told you we knew each other when we were in college? Well, we actually were *really* good friends. We spent lots of time together, your mom and me. In fact, there was a time we talked about getting married. Only…only it just didn't work out."

Heather's gray eyes watched him without blinking.

Daniel could feel beads of perspiration forming on his forehead. He should have thought this through better. Just how did you explain something like this to a ten-year-old? Did she understand the facts of life, all about the birds and bees and so forth? Just how much was enough?

"Honey?" Monica said, drawing her daughter's gaze. Her voice was once again gentle, controlled. "You know how sometimes you ask questions, and I tell you you're too young to understand and that I'll explain when you're older? I've decided you're old enough to know something now that I've never told you before."

"Okay."

Monica lifted her eyes toward Daniel. The look was brief, and yet it was long enough for him to wonder how different his life might have been had he married her, stayed in Boise, raised not only Heather but other children, too.

She looked at Heather once again. "Heather, Daniel is your father."

The house seemed deathly quiet. He could hear the ticking of the sweep-second hand on his watch.

Slowly Heather turned her head so she could look at him. "You're my dad?"

He nodded.

"Honest?"

"Honest."

"Why haven't you come to see me before?"

He opened his mouth, but no words came out. He didn't know how to answer that question.

Monica answered for him. "Because I never told him about you."

Confusion, hurt, hope. He saw it all in Heather's eyes as she stared at him. It made him feel overwhelmingly inadequate.

"So do you wanna see me now that you know?"

"Yes," he answered solemnly. "I do want to see you. I hope you'll spend lots of time with me this summer."

She worried her lower lip with her teeth. Her eyes narrowed in thought. Finally she asked, "Can I call you Daddy?"

The simple question caused a rush of emotion unlike anything he'd experienced before. If he tried for a hundred years, he'd still be unable to define it. "Sure. I'd like that. I'd like it a lot."

"And are you gonna come to the carnival on Friday with us?"

He glanced over at Monica. She nodded her head.

"I'll be there," he told Heather. "You can count on it."

She looked at her mother. "Can I go call Mary and tell her about my dad?"

"I suppose it would be all right."

Quickly Heather was off the sofa and out of the room, disappearing up the stairs. Her bedroom door closed behind her, then silence. Again, Daniel heard the ticking of his watch.

"That wasn't so bad," he said after a lengthy pause.

"No."

He turned toward Monica again. She was frowning. "What's wrong?"

"It isn't going to be that easy, Daniel. We shouldn't fool ourselves into thinking it will be."

"But she seemed okay with—"

"She's just a little girl. It's going to take time to work things through."

He heard what she was telling him. He didn't know Heather the way she did. He couldn't possibly understand how the girl was going to react to this or anything else.

Would he ever know? Or was it already too late?

Chapter Six

Monica watched her daughter closely over the next few days, but it appeared she'd worried needlessly. Heather seemed delighted to have Daniel for a dad. In fact, if she were perfectly honest, Monica would have to admit she was more than a little jealous by how quickly Heather acclimated herself to having two parents instead of just one.

Daniel arrived at the Fletcher house every day that week, shortly after the school bus discharged Heather and its other riders at the corner. Instead of sharing her day with her mom, as had been their habit since Heather started kindergarten, Heather shared the details with her dad. The two of them sat at the kitchen table, looking so alike with their matching black hair and gray eyes and heart-stopping grins.

Monica understood her daughter's excitement, but she

still felt left out. Excluded. And she was ashamed of herself for feeling that way.

On Thursday, Daniel arrived early, showing up at the door with several bags of groceries in his arms. "You've fed me every night this week," he said in explanation. "I decided it's time I returned the favor."

"You're cooking?"

"Do I detect skepticism in your voice, Ms. Fletcher?"

She couldn't help herself. She laughed.

He stepped around her. "I'm wounded to the quick." His retort was softened by a chuckle.

"Sorry." She followed him into the kitchen. "What are you fixing? Wieners and beans?"

He set the bags on the counter, then turned to look at her. "I thought you liked wieners and beans."

For an instant, it seemed they were back in their old apartment near the Boise State campus. They were struggling to make ends meet plus find enough hours in each day to work and study and still spend time with each other. They'd eaten wieners and beans—an affordable meal—by candlelight more than once back then.

And afterward, they'd often made love on the floor in front of the small gas fireplace.

Suddenly breathless, she turned toward the cupboard. "I'll set the table."

"Monica."

Reluctantly she faced him again.

He stepped closer. "I wish you'd stop being nervous around me."

"I can't help it." She shrugged and tried to smile.

"Why?"

"You *know* why. I'm worried about Heather. This…having a dad around…is all new and different to her. At the moment, she's excited by the novelty of it.

But there are serious issues we haven't discussed yet. We still have so much to work out before you go back to Chicago in the fall.'' Monica stopped, swallowed the lump in her throat, then added, ''She's going to hate it when you leave. She loves you already, Daniel.''

''I love her, too. And I know we've got lots of things to work out.'' He moved even closer. ''But is that the only reason?''

''Reason for what?'' She was held mesmerized by his gaze.

''For you being nervous around me.'' He leaned toward her.

''Nervous?''

His voice lowered a notch. ''I'd like very much to kiss you, Ms. Fletcher.''

Her heart was pounding like a jackhammer. ''I don't think that's a good idea.''

''Maybe. Maybe not.'' His lips brushed lightly over hers.

Oh, she was positive it wasn't a good idea. It made her think things she shouldn't be thinking. It made her remember things she shouldn't be remembering.

He cradled her face between his hands, tilting her head slightly as he pressed his mouth more firmly against hers. The kiss was sweet, tender, alluring. Instinctively she rose on tiptoe, drawing closer to him. She felt the unmistakable stirring of pure, unadulterated desire coiling inside her.

And then the front door slammed. ''Mama, I'm home. Where's Dad?''

Monica jumped out of his embrace. A guilty heat rushed into her cheeks.

''We're in the kitchen,'' Daniel called in reply.

Heather appeared a moment later. She dropped her

backpack on the counter, then kicked off her shoes and slid them under the end table beside the family room sofa. "Guess what happened at school today?"

Daniel grinned at their daughter. "Couldn't possibly guess. Tell us."

Heather launched into her story, but Monica didn't hear a word of it. Her thoughts lingered on Daniel's kiss. Why had he done it? Unconsciously she touched her fingertips to her lips. Why had she reacted the way she had? It was only a kiss.

She cast a surreptitious glance in his direction.

She supposed a woman always harbored some remnants of feeling for the father of her child, no matter what else happened in the relationship. Was that what that kiss had been? Just a kind of nostalgia?

Daniel burst out laughing, and Heather did the same. The joyful sound filled the kitchen, making it feel warm and cozy. Like a family.

Monica would be making a terrible mistake to allow herself to fall under the spell of Daniel's considerable charms. He still had his life in Chicago and she had hers here. She could only be hurt if she pretended there was anything else between them other than a mutual concern for Heather.

Daniel's jambalaya—made with ham, smoked sausage, onions, celery, bell peppers and rice and seasoned with bay leaves, mustard, cumin, garlic and thyme— brought rave reviews from mother and daughter alike. Daniel was particularly pleased and amused by Monica's surprise that he'd learned to cook something beyond wieners and beans in the last decade.

After supper, father and daughter did the dishes, then Daniel helped Heather with her homework, a task he found as delightful as everything else he did with her. When Monica announced it was Heather's bedtime, he knew it was a not-so-subtle hint for him to say goodnight and depart, but he pretended not to understand. He wasn't ready to leave just yet. Only a small, silent house awaited him. He preferred to stay here...with Monica.

There was no denying the attraction that had crackled between them all evening. He felt it whenever they were close. He thought she must feel it, too, judging by the wary look in her eyes.

That kiss had changed things.

It didn't help that he remembered—in every wonderfully specific detail—what it was like to make love to Monica Fletcher. But why did the memory affect him as it did? It wasn't as though he'd lived like a monk in Chicago. There'd been other women in his life through the years. He'd even been engaged to one of them. But right at this moment, he couldn't think of any of their names or even what they'd looked like. He knew, beyond a doubt, it had been a long time since a simple kiss had affected him this much.

Monica returned to the kitchen after seeing Heather to bed. She glanced nervously at Daniel before retrieving a bottle of chilled water from the refrigerator.

He watched her tip her head back and swallow. He found the arch of her delicate white throat enticing and wanted nothing so much as to trace tiny kisses down its length, to feel her pulse against his lips, to taste her skin with the tip of his tongue.

She lowered her head, met his gaze across the room, and he knew she'd read his thoughts by the way her eyes widened, knew she felt the same pull of attraction simmering between them. It would be so easy...

"You should go, Daniel."

He rose from his chair. "You feel it, too."

"Yes."

"Then don't you think we should find out what—"

"No, I don't."

"But why not?" He took a step forward. "We're both adults."

She stiffened. "There are other things to think about. It would only confuse Heather if we were to get involved beyond what we are now. Besides, we're too different, you and I. We've always wanted different things."

"We've changed."

"Not that much."

"How do you know?" He took another step toward her. "Maybe—"

"What do you want from me? Sex?" She glared at him with accusing eyes, and her voice and body shook with unmistakable anger. "Find somebody else, Daniel. I'm not a naive twenty-year-old with stars in her eyes any longer. I've learned I have to live with the decisions I make, good or bad, right or wrong. I don't intend to make another wrong one when it comes to you. The last one cost me too dearly."

He winced. "I guess I deserved that."

She turned her back toward him, but not before he'd caught the sudden glimmer of tears.

He swore beneath his breath. He hadn't meant to make her cry. He felt like a jerk.

Slowly he headed for the hall. In the doorway, he stopped and looked in Monica's direction. "I'm sorry. You're right. This is about Heather, not you and me. I'll keep that in mind from now on."

Monica heard the front door close behind him as he left. The sound made her flinch.

She hadn't wanted him to leave. She'd wanted him to grab her and kiss her and tell her he didn't care about being sensible. That he wanted her. That he *cared* for her.

"He's only here for the summer," she whispered aloud. "Only for the summer."

She didn't draw comfort from that reminder as she'd hoped. It only made her feel worse.

The truth was, she was getting used to Daniel's company. No, not just used to it. She looked forward to it...she *wanted* it.

And it wasn't merely nostalgia for what they had once shared. This was something new.

It was also something dangerous.

For the first time in over a decade, Monica felt that her heart could be at risk, and she was scared to death of what the result might be.

"What's wrong with you today, Fletch?"

Monica glanced up from her day planner to look at Doug Goodman, the head of Solutions' accounting department.

He raised a hand. "Don't try to say, 'Nothing.' We've worked together too long for that."

She offered an apologetic smile. Doug always had been able to read her moods.

Back when Solutions was expanding beyond a home-based business, she'd hired him. Before his first week of employment was out, he'd asked her out on a date. After a great deal of persuasion on his part, she'd accepted. She'd found him warm and funny, and she'd enjoyed his company immensely. But it had become quickly apparent she was never going to take a serious interest in him. Not in the romance department. After a while, they'd become trusted friends.

"It's Heather," she answered him now.

"Is she sick?"

Monica shook her head. "It's her father."

That made Doug sit up and take notice. "Her father?" His expression changed from concern to curiosity. He'd always understood this topic was out of bounds, and he'd honored her silence. But that didn't mean he wasn't interested.

"I...I've told her who he is. In fact, they've met each other."

"And?"

She rose from her chair and walked to the window. "And they're getting along quite well."

He tapped the tip of his pencil against the palm of his hand, waiting. Doug was a very patient man.

Monica glanced over her shoulder. "Daniel Rourke," she said in answer to his unspoken question.

"*The* Daniel Rourke? The writer?" He whistled. "You sure know how to keep things close to your vest, Fletch."

"We were engaged in college." She paused, then added, "He never knew about Heather. I never told him I was pregnant."

Doug came to join her at the window. He put an arm around her shoulders and gave her one of his searching looks. "This has got you tied in knots, doesn't it?"

She felt ridiculously close to tears.

He cupped her chin with his hand, tilting her head back, forcing her to meet his gaze. "I see," he said after a long silence.

And she was afraid he did.

"Fletch, I always wondered why you didn't fall head

over heels for me.'' He gathered her closer, let her press her face against his best suit, even though he knew she was going to cry.

Her reply was muffled. ''Accountants were never my type.''

''Yeah, I know.'' He kissed the top of her head.

The tears came in earnest then. She sobbed quietly while Doug stroked her hair and murmured comforting promises that all would turn out well. It didn't matter if either of them believed the words. It was enough just to say and hear them.

At long last, she drew back from the solace of his embrace. She sniffed, then offered him a weak smile. ''I hope I didn't ruin your suit.''

''So do I.'' He leaned over and grabbed a tissue from the box on her desk. ''Here. You need this. You never look your best with black stuff under your eyes.''

''Thanks a bunch.''

''Don't mention it.''

While Monica tried to remove the smudged mascara with the tissue, Doug returned to the chair on the opposite side of her desk. He didn't say anything until she sat down on her own chair.

''So what are you going to do about it?'' he asked.

''About what?''

''About these feelings you've got for Mr. Rourke.''

''I don't know.'' She looked at her hands, folded atop her desk. ''Nothing probably.''

He leaned forward. ''That would be a mistake.''

''There's no future for us, Doug. Daniel never wanted the same things I did. He didn't want a home and family. He wanted success, and that's what he got. He went off to Chicago and made a name for himself.''

''But he's here now, isn't he?''

"Only for a few months."

"Are you still in love with him?"

Her pulse quickened as she looked at her friend. "How could I love him? Until two weeks ago, I hadn't seen him in eleven years. I don't even know who he is now."

"Maybe this is something new." He shrugged. "There's such a thing as love at first sight."

"Not for me," she whispered.

He waited a few moments, then asked, "Are you sure, Fletch? Are you real sure?"

Are you sure, Fletch? Are you real sure?

Monica stared at her reflection in her bedroom mirror while Doug's words echoed in her mind for the thousandth time that day. As always, her silent reply was, No. No, she wasn't sure. She didn't know what she thought or felt or wanted.

But love at first sight?

It wasn't a possibility. It couldn't be. Otherwise, she would have fallen victim to it years ago. It wasn't as if she hadn't had opportunities. It wasn't as if there hadn't been men willing to get serious. Yet Monica had never felt drawn to any of them. Not even to Doug, who was one of the nicest, sweetest, most intelligent guys she'd ever known.

But now, here was Daniel, and suddenly she was feeling and thinking like an emotional teenager. It was crazy. She was too practical for such nonsense. She'd stopped believing in happily ever after and other fairy-tale endings long ago.

Certainly she'd stopped believing in Daniel Rourke, she reminded herself.

The reminder didn't help.

She turned away from the mirror, and her gaze fell on the copy of Daniel's book on her night table. She walked across the room, picked up the book and turned it over to stare at the photo on the back of the dust jacket. Her heart fluttered as Daniel's image stared up at her.

She'd been reading his book at bedtime. It was good. Daniel was more than just a competent writer. The case was one of those sensational ones that had drawn media attention from around the world, and many writers had covered it adequately. But it was Daniel's extraordinary talent that had made his articles so hugely popular at the time and this book such a blockbuster hit now. His writing provoked her to look at things in a new light. It caused her to seek to understand different points of view. It drew her into the emotional part of the story while still forcing her to look objectively at the facts.

She'd never guessed, back in college, that he would be this good.

"I don't even know who you are, Daniel. How could I possibly be falling in love with you again?"

The ringing of the doorbell interrupted her thoughts before she could mentally form any sort of response.

"I'll get it!" Heather yelled. A moment later, she called, "It's Daddy. Are you ready?"

Monica put the book down, then looked once again in the mirror. "Am I ready?" she asked her reflection.

"Mama?"

"I'm coming." With a deep breath, she reached for her purse and headed out of her room.

Daniel was waiting at the bottom of the staircase, leaning casually against the banister while he listened to Heather's excited chatter. When he heard her footfall, he glanced up. A hint of a smile curved the corners of his mouth.

She smiled back at him, unable to keep herself from thinking how handsome he looked. He was wearing tan cotton trousers and dark brown loafers. His pale yellow, short-sleeved shirt looked good against the tanned skin on his arms. Was it any wonder women had made such a fuss over him at his book signing two weeks ago?

Just enjoy tonight, a small voice in her heart commanded. Don't think about it. Just enjoy it.

"You look terrific," Daniel told her, admiration twinkling in his gray eyes.

"Thanks. So do you."

"Are you ready?"

"Ah-huh."

He looked over at Heather. "You know, squirt, it's been over twenty years since I went to a school carnival. Back then, I wouldn't've been caught dead going with a couple of girls." He winked. "Guys sure can be stupid." He offered his left arm to his daughter. As he turned toward Monica, he added, "Can't they?"

She couldn't help laughing. "They sure can, Mr. Rourke."

Daniel had vowed to himself last night that he wouldn't do anything to spoil this evening, not for Heather or Monica. He was determined to be as charming, good-humored and gentlemanly as he knew how while still not crossing the invisible line in the sand Monica had drawn between them.

The elementary school halls were jam-packed with people of all ages, from toddlers to octogenarians. Like the surge of the tide, people were pushed and pulled from one classroom to another. Daniel hadn't been in this much of a crush since the day of the Henderson verdict.

"They're doing face painting in here," Heather announced as she tugged on his hand. "Come on."

He followed his daughter into the room. Three artists were painting the cheeks of children. A sign announced numerous choices of design. "What are you going to get?" he asked Heather.

"I can't get one before I read my story at the ceremony. Mrs. Connolly, the principal, said we couldn't. But you can."

He shook his head. "Hey, I don't think—"

"Come on, Daddy," she pleaded. "It'll be cool."

He looked to Monica for help but found none. She was too busy trying to suppress her laughter...and failing miserably.

"They've got a pirate," Heather continued. "How 'bout that one?"

He raised an eyebrow at Monica.

She gave him an innocent look. "Oh, I think you'd look very handsome with a pirate painted on your cheek. We'll ask for a yellow bandanna to match your shirt. It'll be dashing."

"Gee, thanks." He turned back toward Heather, meaning to refuse, but the words died in his throat. She looked so darn eager. "Ah, what the heck," he muttered.

A few minutes later, he was seated on a child-size chair, trying to hold completely still, as instructed by the girl painting his face, while Monica and Heather hovered nearby, both of their faces wreathed in smiles.

If Charley could see me now, he thought. But even if he could see, his editor would never believe it. More than once, Charley Cooper had told Daniel he was too serious, that he was sorely lacking in a healthy sense of humor whenever he was working on a story.

"My goodness. It *is* you. You're Daniel Rourke."

He turned his head toward the woman's voice—and got a yellow stripe of face paint across the bridge of his nose for his trouble.

"Oh," the woman—an attractive brunette with large hazel eyes, a lush mouth and generous other attributes—continued, "I'm so sorry. That was my fault." She thrust out her hand. "I'm Becky Stover, Mary's mother."

"Nice to meet you." He wiped the paint off his nose with a paper towel before shaking her hand.

"I'm terribly sorry for interrupting. It's just that…well, I was hoping to get your autograph. I brought a copy of your book with me, just in case you were here tonight. Would you mind signing it?"

Book and pen appeared suddenly and were thrust into his hands. Seeing no polite way to refuse, he opened the book to its title page and scribbled his signature.

Becky Stover glanced at Heather. "When Mary told me about your dad, I thought she was trying to pull a fast one on me." She turned a dazzling smile in Daniel's direction. "If ever I can return the favor…" Her words trailed into a suggestive silence as she held out her hands and took back the book and pen.

"No problem," he replied.

"Excuse me, won't you? I really must go find my children. Thanks again."

"Sure." He returned her smile, but inwardly, he was thinking, Overeager divorcée. Since starting his book tour this spring, he'd learned to spot one at forty paces.

"I'm finished, sir," the artist said, interrupting his thoughts.

He nodded to the girl, quickly forgetting the pushy Ms. Stover. "Thanks." He rose, then took hold of Monica's arm. "Your turn."

"Oh, no. I—"

"Fair's fair."

"But, Daniel, I—"

"Do it, Mama. Get one just like Daddy's."

"Yeah," Daniel said as he pressed gently on her shoulders with his hands, forcing her into the chair. "Get one just like mine."

Her pretty brown eyes narrowed as she looked up at him. "Payback, huh?"

"Yeah. Payback." He grinned. "And it's sweet, Ms. Fletcher. Real sweet."

Chapter Seven

Monica forgot to be worried or anxious and, instead, enjoyed each and every moment of the evening. Daniel maintained a friendly, yet dispassionate attitude toward her, much to her relief.

From the face painting, where Monica had acquired a yellow-and-red parrot on her right cheek, they went to the cake walk. Heather won a triple-decker fudge cake with bright pink frosting. Monica and Daniel came away empty-handed. After that, they proceeded to the fish-pond. Monica caught a kewpie doll. Heather snagged a stuffed bear. Daniel reeled in a bag of plastic green soldiers.

"I didn't know they still made these," he marveled as he looked at the tiny toys in the palm of his hand. "I used to play with the ones my dad had as a kid. Looked just like these."

An announcement over the P.A. drowned out whatever Monica started to reply.

Heather grabbed for her parents' hands. "It's time for the program. Come on. I want you to have good seats." With that, she dragged them out into the crowded hallways.

Monica glanced over at Daniel above Heather's head. She found him watching her. He was smiling. So was the pirate on his cheek. She smiled back, a feeling of joy bubbling up in her chest.

This was what it was supposed to be like.

Heather half lead, half dragged her parents toward the front of the auditorium. They managed to get seats in the fifth row center. "I'm supposed to be backstage," she told them as they sat down. "I'd better hurry."

"Break a leg," Daniel called.

She stopped long enough to turn and grin at him.

The smile nearly stopped Monica's heart. Heather looked so completely happy. No matter what else happened this summer, she would always remember her daughter's expression tonight. She would always remember the smile Daniel had put there.

She could have loved him for that alone.

Don't go there, she warned herself silently. It would only bring her sorrow down the road if she did.

Mrs. Connolly walked onto the stage and raised her hands for silence. It took the crowd of parents and children a while to comply, but eventually, they did so.

"Good evening, everyone. We're so glad you could join us for tonight's festivities. Before we know it, we will be taking our summer recess—" She was interrupted by a loud cheer from the children. She smiled tolerantly and waited for them to quiet down before continuing. "As is our custom, tonight we are honoring the achievements of a number of our students."

Over the years, Monica had attended numerous school programs, pageants, and carnivals. She had sewn costumes and baked cookies and cakes and painted posters. She had enjoyed every occasion, but tonight was special...because Daniel was with her.

She glanced his way. The pirate on his cheek seemed to wink at her as if even he knew what a unique evening this had turned out to be.

She'd been such a dreamer as a girl. She'd believed in happy endings, and she'd wanted one for herself. She'd thought Daniel would give it to her. He hadn't, and so she'd stopped believing. She would be a fool to start believing again.

Wouldn't she?

Daniel sat forward in his seat, and Monica knew Heather must have walked onto the stage. But it was Daniel she continued to watch, even as she heard their daughter begin to read her story. She recognized the delight in his eyes.

She hadn't expected him to be such a caring father. She hadn't expected him to want to be involved. Was it only because he was on sabbatical? Would he forget Heather—and Monica—when he went back to Chicago?

She wanted to believe in him, she realized. She had already taken an enormous risk, just telling him about Heather, but that had been because she'd known it was the right thing to do. She hadn't felt she had any other choice. But now her heart seemed to be asking her to take another risk. Could she do it?

Daniel started to applaud as he glanced her way and grinned. "She's great!" he said. "Really great."

Monica could only nod.

Mrs. Connolly returned to the stage, and once again raised her hands for silence. "Thank you, Heather. That was lovely." Her gaze swept over the audience. "It seems Heather has been blessed genetically with her writing talent. I have just been informed that her father is with us tonight. Mr. Rourke, would you be kind enough to join Heather on our stage?"

Daniel muttered something beneath his breath before getting to his feet. If he wasn't happy about this, one wouldn't have guessed. He wore a gracious smile as he made his way to the aisle and then up to the stage.

"May I introduce Heather's father, Mr. Daniel Rourke," Mrs. Connolly said as he climbed the steps. "I'm sure you're all aware of Mr. Rourke's enormously successful book, *And The Rich Kill,* which just reached number two on the bestseller list. What many of you may not know is that he's a Boise State graduate and a native Idahoan."

More applause followed. Monica watched as Daniel put his arm around Heather's shoulders and gave her a smile. Heather smiled back.

"Mr. Rourke, would you care to share a few words with us?" Mrs. Connolly held the microphone out to him.

"I'd just like to say I'm enormously proud of my daughter. It was a real treat, being here tonight and getting to hear her read her work out loud."

"I think many of us would like to hear how you came to write your book. It isn't often we have such an opportunity."

His dark brows drew together in a small frown as he looked at the principal. "I doubt anybody's interested in that, Mrs. Connolly." There was a reproving edge in his voice. "They came to hear the kids. Not me."

Before Mrs. Connolly could say anything further, he left the stage, Heather tagging along, still holding his hand.

Monica could have kissed him. She couldn't believe a school principal would forget the children, but that's exactly what the woman had done. *Daniel* hadn't forgotten.

Yes, she could have kissed him.

Daniel tried to focus on the remainder of the program, but he could feel the stares of others on the back of his neck. A sixth sense told him the earlier interruption by Mrs. Stover with a book for him to sign was going to seem like a pleasant interlude before this evening was over.

His suspicions turned out to be correct. When the program was finished, he barely had a chance to rise to his feet before there was a crowd of people pressing in around him, asking questions about the trial and his book and where he'd grown up in Boise and who were his folks and what was he going to write next and countless other questions. He tried to put them off with a few, brief answers, but it didn't seem to satisfy. They just kept asking.

He glanced over his shoulder. Monica and Heather had disappeared from view, squeezed out by the crowd. He thought of a few choice words he'd like to say to Mrs. Connolly. And after he said them, he'd like to ring her neck. The evening had been going well, he'd thought, right up until the moment the principal had made a big deal about who Heather's dad was.

"Listen, folks," he said, hoping he didn't sound as angry as he felt, "if you don't mind, I'd just like to enjoy the rest of the carnival with my daughter and her mother.

You'll have to excuse me." He forced his way between two overweight women.

His gaze scanned the auditorium, looking for Monica and Heather. He found them standing in a corner, talking to a tall, thin man who was scribbling in a small notepad. The fellow had *reporter* stamped all over him.

Daniel muttered another curse as he strode toward them.

"Sorry about that," he said as he stepped up to Monica's side. A quick glance into her eyes, and he could tell she was upset.

The reporter turned toward him. "Hello, Mr. Rourke. I'm Garth Johnson of the *Boise Herald.* Would you mind answering a few—"

"Yes, as a matter of fact, I would mind." He took hold of Monica's arm. "Let's go."

Their exit from the school reminded Daniel of the times he'd watched famous people, from presidents to rock stars, dashing for waiting limos or rear entrances of hotels while reporters and fans clamored for their attention. Of course, he and Monica and Heather weren't being pursued, but the feeling was there, all the same.

As soon as the doors of his automobile closed, he breathed a sigh of relief, then muttered, "Sorry," again.

"It wasn't your fault," Monica replied.

Maybe not, but he still felt responsible. He glanced into the back seat. "I thought your story was great, Heather. Really great."

"Thanks, Daddy." Of the three of them, Heather was the only one who didn't seem upset. "Did you like Mary's poem, too?"

"I sure did."

Daniel turned the key in the ignition and started the car. In silence, they drove out of the parking lot.

Dusk had fallen over the city while they'd been in the school. Streetlights were just beginning to automatically turn on. The evening air was cool and sweet with the smells of springtime.

On Overland Road, a souped-up Chevy with the truck bed full of teenagers roared past them, doing a good ten miles an hour over the speed limit. One of the boys, no older than sixteen, raised a beer can in a type of salute.

Stupid kids, Daniel thought. Then he glanced in the rearview mirror at Heather. Her eyes were closed, and it looked as if she was asleep.

His daughter would celebrate her eleventh birthday in less than four months. In another five years she could be one of those girls in the back of a speeding truck.

The thought hit him like a fist in the solar plexus.

How did a parent protect a child from such things? His dad couldn't have stopped him, even if he'd tried. It was nothing short of a miracle that Daniel had lived past the age of fifteen. He'd pulled some mighty dumb stunts in his day.

"You pray a lot," Monica said in a soft voice, answering his unspoken question.

He glanced quickly at her, then back at the road.

"That's the only way I know to cope," she continued. "Otherwise, I'd go crazy with worry. There's so much that can go wrong. You just do the best you can, make the best decisions you can make at the time."

"I never gave it much thought. How hard it is to be a parent, I mean. Not just the time and money it takes, but the emotional investment. My dad… Well, he never noticed how I was growing up. He just let my stepmoms take care of me and figured I'd turn out okay in the end."

"Is that why you didn't want to have a family of your own?"

Daniel frowned. "Maybe." He tossed another quick glance in her direction. "I loved my dad, you know. In spite of his faults, I loved him."

"Most of us love our parents, no matter what."

He turned into Monica's subdivision, slowing to twenty miles per hour as he followed the meandering street past homes with well-groomed lawns. Light spilled through windows as darkness gathered, creating warm clusters of gold.

Daniel supposed Monica was right. He supposed most people loved their parents in spite of their faults. Because who was perfect? Certainly he wasn't.

"Heather's always going to love you, Daniel."

The car came to a stop in front of her house. He cut the engine, then turned toward her. "Are you reading minds now? That's twice in the last ten minutes you've known exactly what I was thinking."

Her smile was tender as she shook her head in denial.

He exhaled slowly. "I didn't know it would matter quite this much. Being a parent. I want to be a good father to her."

"I know you do."

"How do I do that from Chicago?"

Monica was silent a long time before answering, "I don't know, but you'll find a way."

He looked toward the back seat. "Out like a light, isn't she?"

"Yes. She sleeps soundly. She always has."

She always has.

But Daniel didn't know that about her because he hadn't been around to find out. He wanted to blame Monica for it, but the truth was, he probably would have gone off to Chicago anyway, even if he'd known she was pregnant. He probably would have walked out on Monica and his responsibility to her.

It was an unpleasant admission to make, even just to himself.

"I'll carry her to her room." He sounded gruff.

"You don't have to. I can wake her. Kids always fall right back to sleep."

He reached for the door latch. "No, I'd like to."

A few moments later, Monica watched as Daniel carried Heather up the stairs. "Her nightgown's under her pillow," she called after him in a stage whisper.

She waited until the bedroom light went on, then she went into the kitchen and filled the coffeemaker reservoir with water. In a matter of minutes, the room began to fill with the friendly scent of percolating coffee.

Monica grabbed two mugs from the cupboard and set them on the counter, then walked to the kitchen window and looked outside.

She wasn't ready for the evening to end, she realized with some surprise. Almost despite herself, she'd had a good time with Daniel at the carnival. She'd forgotten how he could make her laugh when he wanted to.

"Smells good."

She turned as he stepped into the kitchen. "It's decaf. Would you like some?"

"Sure."

"I thought we could sit on the patio. It's such a nice evening."

"Sounds good."

She returned to the coffeemaker and filled both mugs with coffee. She added a French vanilla flavored creamer to hers, silently offering the same to Daniel by lifting the container toward him while raising an eyebrow in question.

"No, thanks."

As soon as she'd handed him his mug, Monica led the way outside. Cotton bounded up, her entire body wiggling with pleasure. "Stay down, girl," Monica told the dog.

They settled onto two lawn chairs, and for a while, they sipped their coffee in silence, content to stare up at the twinkling stars as they appeared in the night sky. The evening air was balmy, already summerlike.

Monica caught a whiff of lilacs from the large bush in the neighbor's yard. She smiled to herself. There had been a lilac bush in her parents' backyard. As a girl, Monica had liked to pick large bouquets and carry them in to her mother who would then place them in a vase on the dining-room table. Their fragrance would fill the house for hours.

She'd been mighty lucky, she thought now, having Ellen and Wayne Fletcher for parents.

She glanced at Daniel. "You never talked about your dad when we were together. Was he really so indifferent to you?"

"Dad wasn't big on honoring commitment," he replied in a matter-of-fact tone. "Not to any of his wives. Not to his son. Not to any of his employers, either." He didn't sound bitter, just resigned to the truth of his statement.

She waited, instinctively knowing he would continue if she were patient.

"I always wondered if Dad would've been faithful to my mom if she'd lived long enough. Truth is, I don't think so. Dad had a wandering eye, and not just with the ladies. He never liked to stay in one place very long.

Couldn't seem to keep a job longer than a year or two. The only reason he didn't sell the house I grew up in was because of my mother's will. It was her folks' place. She tied it up legally so Dad couldn't sell it or borrow against it. I guess she must've known the truth about him, too.''

I wish you'd told me this years ago, Monica thought as she watched him. She suddenly understood many things she hadn't understood before.

He met her gaze. ''I was always jealous of you and your parents.''

''You were?''

''Sure. The closest I came to having the same thing was with Stephanie. She was Dad's fourth wife, the one who died with him in the car wreck. Stephanie was special. She tried extra hard to give me a good home, to be like a mom to me.'' He shrugged. ''But it was too late by then.''

''Were you ever tempted to get married?'' she asked, her voice falling to just above a whisper. ''After me, I mean.''

He looked up at the night sky, sipped his coffee, stroked Cotton's head with his free hand. After a long while, he answered, ''Once. I met a woman who was as career obsessed as me. Kit was her name. She traveled a lot. Her goal was to get a spot on network news. She'll get it someday. She's smart and pretty and has plenty of drive.''

Were you in love with her?

As if he'd heard the question, he turned toward her again. ''Maybe we were too much alike. Kit and me. Neither one of us invested much of ourselves in the relationship. We both stayed pretty remote, emotionally, even after we decided to get married. Eventually we just drifted apart.''

''How sad.''

One corner of his mouth lifted in a wry smile. ''You know what's really sad? I kept comparing her to you. Kit never could measure up.''

Monica was caught completely off guard by his comment. She couldn't have formed an intelligent reply if her life depended upon it.

Thankfully the moment was broken by the ringing of the telephone. Monica mumbled an apology, then hurried inside to answer it.

Before she could give a greeting, Doug Goodman's voice interrupted her. ''Fletch? Thank goodness you're home.''

''What is it, Doug?'' She could tell by his tone that something was wrong.

''The offices have been burglarized. It's a real mess.''

''Burglarized?''

''The police are here now. You need to come down, Fletch.''

''Of course.'' Her voice cracked over the words. She cleared her throat, then repeated, ''Of course. I'll be there as quick as I can. Doug, do they have any idea who—''

''Not yet. Listen, I've got to go. One of the officers needs to talk to me. Hurry.''

''I will.''

The line went dead.

Monica stared at the receiver a moment before returning it to its cradle. Burglarized? Her offices? How was that possible?

She heard the patio door close and turned around. Daniel was watching her with a concerned gaze.

"What is it?" he asked.

"The office has been broken into. Doug needs me there right away. The police have questions." Her heart was pounding. Her head reeled with the news.

"Would you like me to come along? You could get your mother to stay with Heather, couldn't you?"

It was incredibly tempting to have Daniel accompany her. But if she asked Ellen to stay with Heather, she would have to face another interrogation by her mother about Daniel. She wasn't ready for that. It would be easier to face the police by herself.

"No," she answered at last. "I think it would be better if you stayed here with Heather. If you don't mind?"

"Whatever you need from me."

Maybe later she would find a moment to contemplate his response. Right now, she needed to get downtown.

She headed for the stairs. "You can bed down in the guest room. There's a pair of Dad's pajamas in the bottom dresser drawer if you need them, and there's some new toothbrushes in the top drawer in the guest bath. Just look around and find whatever you need."

"I'll manage fine," he called after her. "You just do whatever you have to do."

Monica grabbed her sweater from the shelf in her walk-in closet. Then she picked up her day planner, grabbed her purse and descended the stairs. Daniel stood at the base. He put his hand out when she reached him, laying it on her shoulder.

"You going to be okay?" he asked.

She nodded, even though her heart still raced. "I don't know why, but I feel frightened. As if the burglar was here or something."

With a nod of understanding, Daniel drew her into his

arms and gave her a reassuring hug. "Call me if you need me," he whispered near her ear.

"Thanks." She swallowed the lump in her throat. Then she added, "I'm glad you were here."

"Me, too, sweetheart."

It was two o'clock in the morning before Monica pulled her minivan into the garage. The weariness she felt went beyond the lateness of the hour. It was something much more internal. It was a sense of violation that weighed so heavily on her heart.

It had seemed like the questions from the police officers would never end. No, Solutions didn't keep anything but petty cash in the office. Yes, nearly all the employees had keys to the main door. No, no one but Monica and Doug knew the combination to the safe. Yes, they were fully insured. No... Yes... No...

She tried not to think of the mess the burglars had left in their wake. She could understand the theft of computers and CD players and fax machines. What she couldn't understand was the need to topple lamps and potted plants and to break picture frames and mirrors. She probably didn't know the worst. Doug had done his best to shield her from it.

With a deep sigh, she slid out of the minivan and went inside. Night-lights lit the hallway and staircase, and she followed their soft glow up to the second floor.

Before going to her own room, she stopped at Heather's. Her daughter lay amidst a jumble of blankets and sheets, her long black hair spreading across the pillowcase like spilled ink. She looked small and innocent, and Monica felt a sudden wave of protectiveness. How could she shelter Heather from the hurts of a cruel and out-of-control world? How could she make sure Heather never knew fear or pain or betrayal?

The answer, of course, was that she couldn't. Not really.

Tears welled in her eyes. She blinked them away, then stepped over to the bed, leaned down and lightly kissed her daughter's forehead.

Heather rolled onto her side, murmuring, "Daddy?"

"No, honey, it's me."

"Mmm."

Monica waited, but Heather was once again sound asleep.

As she left her daughter's room, her gaze fell on the open doorway to the guest room. She was drawn irresistibly toward it.

As with all the rooms in Monica's house, a night-light provided soft illumination. Just enough for her to see the bed and the man in it. Like his daughter, he lay in a jumble of blankets. His right arm formed an arc above his head. His face was turned toward the doorway, the shadow of a beard darkening his cheeks and jaw. Unlike his daughter, his torso was bare, the bedcovers pushed down to his waist. Black hair grew across the width of his upper chest, then narrowed as it dropped to his belly button, disappearing beneath the sheet.

Monica caught her breath at the purely sensual vision he made. She felt a quickening of her pulse, a tightening in her belly. There was no denying it was desire she felt. There was no pretending it was anything else, no matter how much she might have wanted to think otherwise.

His eyes opened, and his gaze locked with hers.

Monica couldn't seem to breathe.

He slowly sat up. "Are you all right?" His voice was low and gravelly with sleep.

She nodded. Then the tears sprang up again. She choked on an unexpected sob. Before she realized he'd moved, he was out of bed, across the room and holding her in a comforting embrace. He stroked her hair with one hand, rubbed her back with the other. His chin rested atop her head. His skin was warm against her cheek. He smelled good, a little bit cologne, a lot masculine. Strong and safe.

"How can I help?" he asked.

You can hold me forever, just like this.

"Monica?"

She swallowed the lump in her throat. "I'll be okay, Daniel." She drew back, just enough so she could look up at him. "Thanks for staying with Heather."

He peered intently into her eyes. "How bad was it?"

"They took several computers, a fax machine, a couple of CD players. I'm not sure what else." She shuddered. "It's the unnecessary destruction that's the worst part. The thieves seemed to take pleasure in breaking things. I'll have to go back in the morning. There'll be plenty of cleanup to do, and I'll have to help Doug do a complete inventory."

"Need me to stay with Heather?"

"Do you mind? She has dance lessons on Saturday mornings. I could ask Mother."

"No, I don't mind. I want to." He stroked her cheek with his fingertips. "You sure you're okay?"

She caught a ragged breath, reacting to the tender caress. No, I'm not all right. "Yes, I'm fine," she lied.

The air crackled, suddenly charged by a new awareness of each other. She could see the desire smoldering in his eyes, knew he wanted her.

She wished she could slide her hands up his chest, run

her fingers through the course, dark hair that grew there, feel the muscles beneath the surface. She wished...

No, she didn't wish it. She *couldn't* wish it. She had made that mistake before. She didn't want to make it again.

"Monica?"

She shook her head, then said, "Good night, Daniel," and hurried toward the safety of her room, leaving him standing in the doorway, watching her rapid retreat.

Chapter Eight

It was his stomach that awakened Daniel from a sound sleep.

At first he thought he was dreaming about bacon and eggs, but then he realized the breakfast scents were real. He opened his eyes and sat up, for a moment disoriented. Then he remembered where he was. Monica's house. He also remembered what had kept him awake for so long in the middle of the night.

Daniel threw off the covers and slid his feet to the floor. He paused long enough to rake the fingers of both hands through his hair before standing. He yawned and stretched, then made his way into the connecting bathroom. He was in dire need of a hot shower, followed by a cup of coffee in order to clear the cobwebs from his brain.

Monica was right, he told himself a few minutes later as he stood beneath a spray of water. He had no business trying to entice her into his bed, no matter how mutual the desire might be. What was he offering her, after all?

He worked shampoo into a lather as the question repeated itself over and over again in his head.

Not just what was he offering her, but what did he want for himself? That was the real question. Where was he headed? What did the future hold? He had accomplished plenty in his life. He had an interesting job, financial security. Still, he knew something was missing. And the more he was around Heather and Monica, the more he wondered if they weren't a clue to filling that empty place within himself.

But Monica wasn't the sort of woman a man had a casual affair with. She wanted more. She wanted commitment. She wanted promises. She wanted forever.

He'd always thought she wanted too much.

But now...

Gads, what was he thinking? She *did* want too much. Hadn't he proven that he was the last guy who would form a lasting relationship with anyone? As the old saying went, the acorn hadn't fallen far from the tree. Like father, like son. Only difference was, Richard Rourke had married the women, then divorced them. Daniel, on the other hand, always got out *before* the wedding ceremony, saving himself the grief of lawyer fees and court costs.

No, Monica was right to want to keep things casual between them. What they'd once had couldn't be resurrected. Friendship would have to be enough.

He turned off the water, grabbed a towel and dried off. He didn't have much choice for clothes to wear, so he donned what he'd worn to the school carnival last night. He figured he could stop by his place and get some clean clothes before he drove Heather to her music lessons or dance lessons or whatever it was he'd promised to take her to this morning.

When he entered the kitchen a short while later, he found Monica loading dishes into the dishwasher.

"Hi, Dad!" Heather called to him from the table. "Wait'll you see the newspaper."

He glanced at Monica. "It made the news?" he asked, referring to the break-in at Solutions.

She nodded. "You still like your eggs over hard?"

"Please." After pouring himself a cup of coffee, he walked to the table and looked down at page two of the *Boise Herald*'s local section. He didn't see what he'd expected. Instead his own publicity photograph stared back at him.

"What's this?" he muttered as he picked up the paper and began to read.

Attendees at the Purple Sage Elementary School's year end carnival and honors program last evening had an unexpected treat in store for them when it was revealed that fifth-grader, Heather Fletcher, is the daughter of the well-known reporter, Daniel Rourke. Mr. Rourke was seen applauding loudly after Miss Fletcher read her short story, entitled *Cotton Summer,* a sort of modern-day fairy tale about a dog.

But it was Mr. Rourke's presence that commanded attention from the moment he was introduced to the crowd of parents and children. Mr. Rourke, author of...

The rest of the article was about his Boise roots, his accomplishments in Chicago, his coverage of the Henderson trial and his book. The last line was a quote from his editor:

"I never knew Daniel had a daughter, but if he does, it's no surprise to me that she's won a writing award."

Garth Johnson must have got Charley out of bed last night to get that quote before the paper went to press.

"Pretty cool, huh?" Heather asked when he looked up. "I've never been in the paper before. Have I, Mama?"

"No, honey, you haven't." To Daniel, Monica said, "Sit down, please. Your eggs are ready." She placed a plate on the table.

He gave her a hard look, noting the dark circles beneath her eyes and the pinched corners of her mouth. Her entire body looked stiff.

"Are you okay?" he asked softly.

She nodded, but he knew it was a lie.

"You don't look like you slept much."

"I didn't."

He wanted to ask if it was because of Solutions or because of him. She didn't give him a chance to do either.

"I told Heather what happened and why you'll be taking her to her lessons. I don't know how long I'll be. Probably all day. You can reach me on my cell phone if you need me. There's a note with all the directions over by the phone."

He put his hand on her shoulder. "We'll be fine. Don't worry about us."

"Okay." She sidestepped out from under his hand.

"I'd better get going." She dropped a quick kiss on top of Heather's head. "Mind your dad."

"I will."

Monica avoided looking at Daniel as she headed toward the hall.

"Hey, Mama."

She stopped and glanced behind her.

"I'm sorry about what happened at work. I hope the police find everything all right."

Monica offered a weak smiled. "Thanks, honey."

Daniel ate his breakfast, accompanied by Heather's bright chatter. It still amazed him how much one little girl could talk. He wondered if they were all as gregarious as Heather or if his daughter was unique.

When they were both finished eating, Daniel cleared the table and put the dishes into the dishwasher. Seeing it was full, he looked for the detergent beneath the sink, then filled the soap dispensers and started the wash cycle. Finally he went over to the telephone and picked up the note of instructions Monica had left for him.

Dance lessons were at eleven. The note told him where her leotards and ballet shoes were and gave directions on how to find the studio. It also said Heather had a project to complete for Sunday school.

No friends over until she's done. No going to a friend's house today at all. Not even Mary's.

"What's your Sunday school project?" he asked.

"I'm doing a poster about the Good Samaritan."

"Need any help?"

"Sure."

This fatherhood stuff was a piece of cake, Daniel thought as his daughter grinned at him. He didn't know why he'd been nervous about it. Heather had been a perfect angel since the day he'd met her. The credit had to go to Monica, of course, but it didn't make Daniel any less proud. He'd never known a more well-behaved child than Heather.

He looked at his watch. "Hey, listen. We need to get your things for dance class together and leave. I've got to stop by my house and change before we go anywhere else."

"I'll go get ready," Heather replied as she hopped up from her chair. Then she dashed out of sight.

Yes, sirree. This fatherhood stuff was a piece of cake.

Monica sat on the floor of the file room, sorting through the papers that had been strewn hither and yon by the intruders. She didn't know whether to cry again or to scream in rage. She wanted to do both.

Doug, bless his heart, had cataloged all the missing equipment and had prepared a document that included all the serial numbers, makes and models, and any other needed information for the insurance company. He'd assured Monica that most of it would be covered.

But no one could reimburse her for the less tangible losses. She no longer felt secure. Instead she felt vulnerable. She couldn't explain it. She only knew it was true.

It didn't help that Daniel's presence had only added to that vulnerability.

As tired as she'd been last night when she returned from the office, she still hadn't been able to sleep. She hadn't been able to shake the image of Daniel lying in bed, his chest bare. She hadn't been able to rid her nostrils of the wonderful scent of him or the feel of his warm skin against her cheek. She wanted him, pure and simple. She wanted him to make love to her.

And she was a fool to want it.

She'd gone over eleven years without feeling a man's body next to her own, she reminded herself, and she'd survived. But then, she had never felt this same temptation.

Besides, it wasn't just the physical desire Daniel had brought back to life within her. It was a desire to love and be loved. To be part of a whole family. To have a husband and, maybe, more children.

"Why did you have to come back, Daniel?" she whispered. "I don't want to deal with this."

But she was going to have to deal with it, she silently admitted. Because Doug was right when he'd suggested she was falling in love with Daniel all over again.

"How's it coming?"

She glanced up. Doug stood in the doorway to the file room. She seldom saw her friend dressed in casual attire. He was much more of a nice-suit-and-tie sort of guy, the kind of man who worked hard and was dependable. He was the sort of man you could count on, a good friend whose word stood for something solid. A man who didn't seek fame or fortune but who had much more "down home" expectations and goals.

Why couldn't I have fallen in love with you? she wondered.

Aloud, she answered him, "It's daunting. Half the stuff I don't know what to do with. I'll have to leave it for Terri and Claudia to figure out, I guess."

"So leave it. You don't have to do it all yourself. No one will expect you to."

"Doug?"

He inclined his head. "Yeah?"

"I'm in love with him."

"I know."

She smiled weakly.

"Have you told him how you feel?"

"No."

"Don't you think you should?"

She covered her face with her hands and lowered her head toward her knees. "I don't know what I should do."

Doug showed his usual patience, waiting quietly while she sorted her thoughts.

Looking up again, she said, "Heather is completely enamored with her dad, with having him around all the time. She's going to be heartbroken when he goes back to Chicago. And he's just as taken with her. But none of it is normal right now." She gave a humorless laugh. "You know how, when you first start to date someone, you only let them see you at your best. Your hair is always perfect and you always dress in your best outfits for your dates and you laugh at their jokes, even if you don't find them that funny."

He smiled but still said nothing.

"Well, that's how it is between the two of them right now. They're both on their best behavior. They're having fun, like a couple of pals. But it isn't real. Being a parent can get messy. What if he finds out he doesn't want anything to do with Heather once it does? Or what if I tell him I love him and *that's* the reason he walks out? Heather could lose her dad because of me."

Doug reached out and took hold of one of her hands. "I think you're borrowing trouble. Give the guy some credit. I don't think you could love him if he didn't have more character than that."

Oh, how she prayed Doug was right.

"Tell him how you feel, Fletch. It's the right thing to do. For everybody concerned."

She squeezed his hand. "Thanks, Doug. You're a good friend."

Daniel found the dance studio without mishap, but he was dismayed to find himself in a small room with a number of students' mothers, Becky Stover among them. Shortly after the girls went off to their lesson, Mrs. Stover confirmed her divorced status and made it clear— just as Daniel had suspected last night—that she was readily available to him, should he be so inclined.

He wasn't.

He spent the hour fending off Becky Stover's blatant come-ons, in addition to answering the fanlike questions of the other women in the room. Although he didn't let on, he wasn't in the best of moods by the time the ballet class let out.

Heather and Mary ran into the waiting room, wearing their tights and leotards and carrying their dance cases.

"Hey, Mom," Mary said, "can Heather come over to our house to play?"

Becky turned sultry brown eyes toward Daniel. "If it's okay with Mr. Rourke."

"Sorry." He shook his head. "Heather's supposed to stay home today."

"Please, Daddy," Heather piped in. "I won't stay over at Mary's too long."

He gave his head another shake. "You know what your mom said. You've got that project for Sunday school to finish. Maybe you could ask Mary to come to your house afterward."

"But it'd be okay for me to go to Mary's if *you* said it was. Please, please, please."

Her eyes looked so big and round and hopeful, it was tough to say no to her. But he did it anyway, figuring

Monica knew best. "Sorry. Come on. We'd better get going."

"But, Daddy!" she wailed.

Becky Stover stepped to his side and placed a hand on his arm. "I really wouldn't mind, Mr. Rourke. I'd be happy to bring Heather to your house, if you'd give me your address."

In a pig's eye, he thought as he met her gaze. "Sorry," he repeated, not bothering to tell her they weren't going to his house. He looked at Heather again. "I said let's go."

"It's not fair!" She stomped a foot for emphasis.

Daniel was losing patience. "*Now,* Heather."

"Mama would let me go if she was here."

"Well, she's not here."

Heather stuck out her chin. Her mouth was pressed into a thin, flat line, and her eyes narrowed as she glared at him. *Make me,* they seemed to say.

He couldn't believe this was happening. Right here in public. Everyone in the room was watching, waiting to see what would happen next, waiting to see how he would handle his daughter's defiance.

Not well, obviously.

"Unless you want to feel the palm of my hand against your behind, you'd better get it out to my car… *Now.*"

Her expression turned from insubordinate to desolation in an instant. With a sob, she turned and fled. In her wake, the waiting room was absolutely silent.

What, he wondered, had happened to the perfect little angel he'd known for the past two weeks?

Daniel made it a point not to meet anybody's gaze as he followed after his daughter. He was fairly certain he'd had a right to feel angry, but at the moment, what he felt was about two inches tall.

So maybe this parenting stuff wasn't a piece of cake after all.

Monica returned home at six o'clock that evening. Even before she opened the door, she recognized the scents of chili powder and hamburger. Once she was in the hallway, she heard the sizzle of meat frying in a skillet. She'd thought she was too tired to be hungry. She'd thought wrong.

Daniel was alone in the kitchen when she entered.

"Hi," she said as she placed her pocketbook on the island counter. "Where's Heather?"

"In her room."

Something in his tone told her all was not well. She turned to look at him.

"Don't ask," he warned.

She glanced toward the stairs.

Daniel must have read her mind. "There's nothing wrong with her. At least nothing that won't be cured when I leave."

So…the honeymoon is over. She wondered what had caused the riff between father and daughter.

He tipped his head toward the skillet. "Tacos. I thought you'd want something to eat. Heather hasn't eaten, either."

"Are you staying?" she asked, despite thinking she shouldn't.

"I need to get home."

He was going to run out on them. At the first sign of trouble, he was leaving. It was a good thing she hadn't let him know what she was feeling. It would be better, easier, this way.

Daniel wiped his hand on a dish towel, then stepped toward her. His brows were drawn together in a frown, and he spoke in a low but firm voice. "It wasn't anything serious. Just a slight difference of opinion. I won." He gave her a halfhearted grin. "At least I think I did."

She wasn't sure whether to smile back at him or not. She wasn't certain what he meant exactly. She'd thought...

He kissed her forehead, then whispered, "You look tired. Maybe I should stay until after supper. Do the dishes for you. I guess my laundry can wait."

"Your laundry?"

He drew her into his arms and kissed her again, this time on the mouth. The kiss was gentle and light, filled with caring tenderness. When he pulled back, he said, "You thought I was leaving because Heather and I had a fight. Didn't you?"

Honesty demanded that she nod.

"I don't give in that easy, Monica."

She couldn't help it. She said, "You did before." She searched his face, trying to gauge his reaction.

"Yeah, you're right. I did before."

"Weren't you ever sorry? Didn't you ever want to call me? Not even once?"

His grip tightened on her arms. "I did call. Remember? You had your mother tell me you never wanted to see or hear from me again."

At first his words didn't make sense. Then, for an instant, she thought he must be lying. And finally, she believed him. "When? When did you call?"

He frowned. "I don't know. It must have been February. Maybe early March. I remember it was snowing outside. Why? Does it matter?"

So that's what her mother had meant about her interference. Daniel had called and Ellen had sent him away.

She closed her eyes. Oh, Mother, what were you thinking? Aloud, she said, "No, it doesn't matter."

"Listen, Monica." He cupped her chin with his fingers, forced her to look up at him. "I'm sorry about the past, but I can't undo it any more than you can. It's what we do from here on out that we have some control over. And one thing I'm not going to do is quit being Heather's dad, even when she's madder than a wet hen at me. Like she is right now." He paused, then asked, "Is that understood?"

For a moment they just stared at each other. And then Monica rose up on tiptoes and planted a kiss on his mouth. She hadn't known she was going to do it. Just suddenly it had seemed like the right thing to do.

The kiss deepened. Daniel gathered her close against him. One of his hands splayed against her nape, the other pressed against the small of her back. She allowed her lips to part, and his tongue slipped through the opening to spar lightly with hers.

I love you. I love you. I love you.

He groaned deep in his throat, and in response, a shiver skittered up her spine.

She tugged at his shirt, pulling it from the waistband of his jeans. Then she slid the palms of her hands upward, over the bare skin of his back. Her hands were cool; his flesh was warm.

The years seemed to melt away. She knew this man, knew his body. She loved him and wanted to be a part of him. But she couldn't let it happen. She realized she couldn't, even through the haze of her desire.

Daniel broke the kiss. He cleared his throat, then whispered, "I don't suppose this is going to end the way I want it to."

Monica released a ragged laugh. "No, I don't suppose it will."

"Heather's upstairs."

"Yes, but there are other reasons, too." She eased herself away from him, seeking a little distance so she could think straight.

He took her hand. "Come here and tell me what they are." He drew her with him into the family room. He sat on the sofa, then pulled her onto his lap.

She immediately slid off, distancing herself once again.

He released a sigh of frustration but didn't reach for her again. "So? Tell me the other reasons."

Tell him how you feel, Fletch. It's the right thing to do. She hoped Doug was right.

"Daniel," she began softly, "I don't want to make the same mistakes I made over a decade ago. We were in love then, you and I, but we wanted different things from life. What I want hasn't changed."

His brows drew together in a thoughtful frown.

"I don't want a lover, Daniel. I don't *need* a lover. I've done very well without one all these years. But I do want love. I want to fall in love, to be in love." *I am in love.* "I'd like to get married. I'd like to spend lots of time with my husband, to have our home be a place of warmth and safety. I'd like more children, God willing."

His expression altered very little as she spoke. She couldn't tell what he was thinking, how he was reacting to her words.

"It would be so easy to go to bed with you, Daniel. To let you make love to me. But it wouldn't be enough and it wouldn't be right. Don't you see? It would never be enough for me. In a few months, you'll go back to

Chicago, and Heather and I will still be here. We'll have to go on with our lives in Boise. If I let myself love you again—" and I already have "—it will only mean more heartache."

The room was too quiet. Her chest ached, and she was certain her heart was breaking.

Finally, his voice so low she could barely hear him, he asked, "*Could* you love me again?"

Tears sprang to her eyes. A lump the size of a softball formed in her throat. She mouthed the word, *Yes,* but no sound came with it.

"Then don't we owe it to ourselves to see if we can work things out?"

She blinked rapidly, trying to clear her vision.

He took hold of her hands, enfolding them between his. "I don't know what any of this means, Monica. I don't know if there's a future for us. But...what I do know is that these last couple of weeks have been special to me, and not just because of Heather. There's something going on between you and me. You know there is. And it isn't just desire, though heaven knows, I want you."

"I want you, too," she confessed, her voice hoarse and low.

"Give us the summer. Let's start over. No preconceptions. Just two people getting to know each other, seeing what will happen next." He stared hard into her eyes. "As if I wasn't Heather's dad. As if we weren't old lovers who didn't make it the last time out."

"But you are. We were."

"Humor me, Monica."

She was terrified. She had kept herself in a safe emotional cocoon for many years. He was asking her to come out of it. He was asking her to take a risk, and she was terrified by the request.

"You said you don't want to make the same mistakes you made a decade ago. Well, guess what, Monica? Neither do I."

She couldn't fight him any longer. It was too late anyway. She had already fallen in love with him a second time. The hurt couldn't possibly be less if he walked out today instead of three months from now. And if there was a chance he might never walk out, then she had to take the risk.

"All right, Daniel," she whispered. "We'll start over. I'll give us the summer."

It would either be the best or the worst decision she had ever made, and Monica didn't have a crystal ball to know which one it would be.

Chapter Nine

The hostess led Ellen and Monica through the bistro toward a table beside the window. The narrow, unpretentious restaurant was located in a restored part of the city, tucked between a movie theater and a trendy clothing store. Monica and her mother frequently came here for their Monday lunches. The food was good, the atmosphere fun, and once the noon lunch crowd had cleared out, it was quiet enough for them to enjoy their visit.

And Monica wanted quiet today...because she had something very important to discuss with her mother.

"I can't believe this has happened on top of everything else," Ellen said as soon as the hostess left them at their table. "First Daniel comes back to Boise after all these years, then that awful article appears in the newspaper and now this robbery. It's too much for one person. It's just too much." She opened her menu and perused it, even though she always ordered the same thing when they came here. "I don't know how you're coping with it all."

"There wasn't anything wrong with that article, Mom. In fact, Heather thought it was—and I quote—'pretty cool.'"

Ellen lowered the menu and looked at her with amazement. "Nothing *wrong* with it? How can you say that? It told the whole world that Daniel is Heather's father!"

"What's so terrible about that?" She was ashamed of her sharp tone, but she didn't try to apologize. "He *is* her father."

Ellen leaned forward and whispered, "But you were never married. Everyone must be wondering—"

"Mom, this isn't the fifties. Hardly anyone notices such things these days."

"That doesn't make it right."

Monica sighed. "No, Mom, it doesn't make it right. But I *did* live with Daniel, and I *did* have his baby." She looked out the window in an effort to hide her irritation.

Tall trees cast lacy shadows across the bricked courtyard below. Shoppers with paper bags and baby strollers and businessmen with suit coats and briefcases strolled along the sidewalk, obviously enjoying the first day of June and the promise of summer that came with it.

"Are you ready to order?"

Monica glanced up at the waitress. The young woman had bright red hair, a silver ring in her nose and a friendly smile.

"I'll have the club sandwich."

Ellen handed the waitress her menu. "And I'll have a cup of the minestrone soup and a fruit plate." She was doing her best not to look askance at the young woman's appearance.

No, it definitely isn't the fifties. The thought caused Monica to smile.

When the two of them were alone again, Ellen straightened in her chair, lifted her chin and said in her no-nonsense voice, "You might as well tell me what you've got stuck in your craw. I can tell you're annoyed with me about something."

Her smile vanished. "Yes, Mom, I am." She searched for the right words. She'd been searching for them ever since Saturday night. But there didn't seem to be any "right words," so she simply blundered forward. "It's about Daniel. He told me something this weekend. It was something you did years ago."

"Something *I* did?"

"He said he called to speak to me, and you told him I didn't ever want to talk to him again. Is it true? He called, and you told him to go away and leave me alone?"

Ellen blanched. She dropped her gaze to the center of the table. "It's true."

"How could you do that, Mom?"

She answered in a small voice. "I was trying to protect you. That's all." She looked up again. "You'd been so horribly hurt by what he did. You hadn't heard from him in over two months and you'd done nothing but cry. I was worried about you. You were thin and pale. You didn't eat enough to keep a bird alive. When he called, you were packing to leave for Salt Lake. You'd already made up your mind to give your baby up for adoption. You'd told me you wouldn't want Daniel to marry you out of pity or obligation. So I thought..." She let her words fade into silence. After a tense moment, she added, "I am sorry, dear. I was wrong to interfere, but

I thought I was protecting you. I hope you can forgive me.''

Monica felt the last dregs of anger drain out of her. All she could feel was deep sadness. Could it have been different? Would Daniel have married her if he'd known? Would they have been happy? The questions could never be answered, of course. There was no undoing the past.

She reached across the table and covered her mother's right hand, patting it gently. "It's okay, Mom. I understand why you did it. Of course I forgive you."

Ellen gave her one of those penetrating looks, so peculiar to mothers. "I was right, wasn't I? You *do* still care for Daniel."

"I don't know what I feel for him," Monica lied. She glanced out the window again, not wanting her mother to see the truth. "It's all very confusing at the moment."

That much, at least, wasn't a lie. It was all very confusing, indeed.

"Are you sure you can't cut this sabbatical thing short?" Charley Cooper's voice sounded as if it was coming through a tunnel. "We need your expertise around here. Ed could use your help on a story he's working on. It's a hot one. Would be even better with the Rourke perspective."

"Get off your speaker phone, will you, Charley?" Daniel replied, ignoring everything else his editor had said. "I can hardly understand you."

Charley's voice was much clearer when he continued, "You didn't answer me. When are you coming back?"

"I told you all along it wouldn't be until September."

"But we need you now."

Daniel closed his eyes as he leaned his back against

the doorjamb. It was easy to imagine Charley, seated at his enormous desk in the office that overlooked the Chicago River and had a view of Lake Michigan. His gray-white hair would be sticking out in all directions from the frequent finger-rakings it received throughout the day. He would invariably be doodling with a blue, felt-tip pen on whatever piece of paper was handy. His wire-rimmed glasses would be perched close to the end of his short, bulbous nose, and his bushy eyebrows would be drawn together in a thoughtful frown.

"Rourke, are you listening to me?"

"I'm listening, Charley, but I'm not going to change my mind, so you can save your breath. I'm staying in Boise for the summer."

Charley muttered something on his end of the line—something undoubtedly colorful and not meant for polite company.

Daniel grinned, enjoying himself.

"I suppose this has something to do with that daughter you've got out there."

"Yeah, it's got something to do with Heather." And with her mother.

"Book tours. Kids. Sabbaticals. Damn fool nonsense, all of it, if you ask me."

Daniel chuckled. "Nobody asked you."

"Yeah, well, you're getting my opinion anyway. You know, today's celebrities are tomorrow's has-beens. You need to get your byline back in the paper. This story Ed's working on is a real—"

"I gotta run, Charley. It was nice talking to you."

Before the receiver hit the cradle, Daniel heard his editor shouting, "Wait a minute, Rourke. I want—"

Click.

That felt good, he decided as he turned away from the telephone. *Real* good.

Daniel had worked for Charley Cooper almost from the moment he'd graduated from Boise State. He liked the crusty old coot, and he respected him. He would put Charley up against any newspaper editor in the world and be certain he'd come out on top. Charley Cooper had a nose for news, as the old saying went.

But Daniel was glad there were seventeen hundred miles between him and his editor. Otherwise, he knew Charley would have him working the beat before nightfall.

Charley Cooper hated it when anybody told him, "No."

Daniel whistled as he headed outside to mow the back lawn. As a kid, he'd hated this chore. He'd done just about anything to get out of it. Strange what a decade of living in apartments and condos—with nary a blade of grass in sight—could do to change a man's mind.

With a quick, fluid motion, he pulled the cord to start the mower's engine. It sputtered, then roared to life. Grinning, he pushed the old Toro toward the back fence, cutting a straight line through the thick green grass.

Of course, mowing the lawn was not the source of his high spirits. Those were due to Monica.

He hadn't seen her since Saturday night. She was swamped by things at the office, trying to get everything up and running after the burglary. But he'd talked to her on the phone yesterday and again this morning, and she'd agreed to go out with him on Friday night. An honest-to-goodness date. Dinner and dancing. Just the two of them. With a bit of luck, the night would come with a full moon to help his cause along.

He hadn't felt this way since he was twenty. If this

was the real thing, if it was meant to last, then he didn't want to let it slip away.

As he worked the mower around the trunk of a maple tree, he thought of Charley's plea for him to return to Chicago. Strange. He really didn't feel the urge to get back. He knew it wasn't because he disliked his work. He didn't. He thrived on it. He was good at it.

He'd taken a total of three weeks vacation in all the years he'd been with the paper, and two of those were only because Kit had dragged him to the Caribbean. She'd threatened to do him bodily harm if he refused to go. But even as they'd sunned themselves on pristine beaches, he'd been thinking about work, chomping at the bit to get back.

Sure, he'd been burned out by the trial and the months it had taken him to write his book, but that wasn't why he didn't want to return to Chicago and his job. Monica was the reason for that. Monica and Heather. He needed to know how they were going to fit into his future.

How... Not if.

He stopped in midstride, then shut off the mower. The sudden quiet was deafening.

How... Not if.

He wasn't wondering *if* he wanted Monica to be with him. He was only wondering *how* they could make it work. He wasn't thinking about getting her into his bed. He was thinking about getting her into his life. Permanently.

Daniel Rourke had fallen in love, and he hadn't seen it coming.

The receptionist gave Monica a particularly bright smile when she saw her get off the elevator. "Hi, Ms.

Fletcher.'' She plucked some slips of paper out of Monica's message slot. ''These are for you.''

''Thank you, Terri.'' She glanced through them. ''No call back from the insurance company?''

''Not yet. But there is something waiting on your desk that I think must be pretty important.'' Before Monica could ask, she added, ''I don't know who it's from.''

Hoping it wasn't another problem she would have to deal with, she pushed through the glass door and headed for her office. She stopped when she saw her personal secretary seated on the floor in the file room.

Claudia Williams glanced up as Monica stepped into the small room. ''I'd like to get my hands on the guys who did this.'' Her tone left little doubt what she would do with the culprits if she caught them.

Monica nodded. ''I know what you mean. But I'm amazed what you've managed to get done in one day.''

''I'm lucky. Most of the papers are easy to identify and get back in the right files.''

''Do you need me to bring someone in to help you?''

''I don't think so,'' Claudia answered as her gaze swept the stacks of papers all around her. ''It would probably take longer to explain what I need than to just do it myself.''

Monica understood that philosophy. It was one she often operated under herself. She also knew it could leave a person feeling overwhelmed and frustrated. ''Okay, but let me know if you change your mind.''

''I will.''

She left the file room and continued toward her office, silently counting off the many things she needed to accomplish before the day was done. She was so far behind now. It didn't help that she'd stayed at lunch with her mother longer than usual. But she was glad they'd had the chance to talk, to clear the air.

Monica opened the door to her office and strode toward her desk, once again glancing through the message forms in her hand. As she drew closer, she caught sight of something on her desk, looked up and came to a sudden halt.

A beautiful cut-glass vase stood in the center of her desk. Rising out of it was a bouquet of calla lilies. Her favorite flower in the world. Their showy spathes were white, pink, purple and yellow. Several of the flowers draped elegantly over the rim of the vase while others stood upright.

Monica's heart tripped, and she caught her breath. She remembered distinctly the last time she'd been given a calla lily. It was the night she'd moved in with Daniel. They'd gone out to dinner, and he'd presented her with a corsage made of one pale pink calla lily. It was all he could afford. Now she was looking at a dozen of them in a single bouquet.

She reached for the small white envelope lying on the desk beside the vase. With trembling fingers, she opened the flap and drew out the card.

"To Monica," it read, "for giving us the summer."

"Oh, Daniel."

He'd remembered. After all these years, he'd remembered about the calla lilies. He'd given her this beautiful bouquet and a summer.

If only she knew what lay beyond September.

She sank onto a nearby chair. She was a coward, she admitted to herself. She'd kept her heart, her emotions, safely under wraps for years. Now she was being asked to set them free, to see what might develop.

And she was afraid.

Afraid because she wanted more than a summer. She wanted beyond September.

She wanted it all.

If Daniel had opened the door and found the president of the United States standing on his front stoop, he couldn't have been more surprised.

"Hello, Daniel," Ellen Fletcher greeted him, her voice quivering slightly. "I hope I haven't come at a bad time."

He glanced down at his sweat-stained tank top, then back at Monica's mother. "No, I just finished cutting the grass." He pushed open the storm door. "Come on in."

"Thank you."

"Make yourself at home," he told her, motioning toward the living room. "I just need a minute to wash up." He hurried toward the bathroom.

While his thoughts churned in his head, wondering what had brought Ellen to his house, he quickly peeled off his shirt. Then he ran water in the sink and freshened up the best he could before donning a clean T-shirt. He was back to the living room before more than five minutes had passed.

Ellen Fletcher sat on the sofa, looking anything *but* "at home." She was perched on the edge of the couch, her hands clasped together and resting on her knees.

When she saw him, she forced a tiny smile and gave a nervous little laugh. "I suppose you wonder why I've come."

"I'm a bit curious, Mrs. Fletcher." An understatement. He sat opposite her in a faded overstuffed chair.

"Well…" She paused, drew a deep breath, then continued, "It's about Monica and Heather, of course."

He arched one eyebrow. If she was about to warn him off, she wasn't going to be pleased with what he said to her in return.

"I...I came to apologize. And to ask your forgiveness."

His surprise must have shown on his face.

She smiled again, this one self-deprecating. "I can see you didn't expect that from me."

"No, ma'am, I didn't."

"Parents want only what's best for their children. When you called...when I told you Monica didn't want to talk to you all those years ago, it wasn't the truth. I didn't even tell her you called. I...I thought I was protecting her from being hurt more than she already had been. But I was wrong. You and she should have had the chance to work things out between you. It wasn't up to me."

Daniel nodded. He'd suspected, since talking to Monica, that Ellen had lied to him in that phone conversation. Now that the older woman had confirmed it, he expected to feel anger, but it didn't come. He supposed because he'd already taken a good hard look at what sort of person he'd been back then and hadn't found a sterling, faultless character looking back at him.

Ellen stood. "I just want you to know I'll not interfere again, Daniel. You have my word on it."

He rose from the chair. "I'm glad of that. And, if it helps any, I don't hold the past against you."

"Thank you," she replied softly, and her face revealed the depth of her relief.

"Mrs. Fletcher, it's probably me who should be thanking you. You and your husband have had a hand in making Heather into the kind of girl she is. I'd like to think I would've been around to help out if I'd known

I had a daughter. But it's her mother and you and Mr. Fletcher who get the credit for how Heather's turned out. She's one terrific kid.''

Ellen tilted her head slightly to one side. ''You've changed.''

''Time'll do that to a guy.''

''Not always for the better.''

''I suppose not.''

''But it has you. For the better, I mean.''

He shrugged, not sure what to say to that.

''I'm glad I came.'' Her smile was more genuine this time. ''I expect I'll be seeing you again.''

He returned her smile, saying warmly, ''I hope you're right, Mrs. Fletcher.''

''Call me Ellen. You're not a college boy anymore.''

There was a lot of meaning behind those simple words, and Daniel was surprised by how much this woman's approval meant to him, now that he had it. He didn't know how to tell her, so he said nothing.

He followed her to the door and watched as she descended the steps and made her way down the walk. It wasn't until she'd gotten into her car and started the engine that he closed the door.

As he turned around, he wondered if Monica knew her mother was coming to see him. He wondered if he should tell her Ellen had been there.

The phone rang, interrupting his musings, and he went to answer it. ''Hello.''

''Hello, Daniel.''

''Monica.'' He grinned. ''I was just thinking about you.''

''I got the flowers. Calla lilies. They're so beautiful.''
Like you.

"You couldn't possibly know how much they mean to me."

"I'm glad." He held the receiver to his ear with his left hand and cradled the mouthpiece with his right, wishing the same hands could be holding and cradling Monica instead.

"It's been years since a man sent me flowers." Her voice was husky.

"Then this town is full of idiots."

She laughed softly. "Thank you for saying so."

"Only saying what's true."

She didn't reply.

He cleared his throat. He thought it better to change the subject before he said too much. "Are things improving at the office? You getting it all organized again?"

"It's better now that Claudia's here. She's an organizational whiz. I'm amazed by what she's accomplished in one day."

"I'd be glad to come down and help if there's anything I could do."

She hesitated, then answered, "That's sweet of you, Daniel."

"But?"

"But it isn't necessary."

"Not ready to answer people's questions about what I'm doing there?"

"I guess that about sums it up."

"Okay. Just wanted to help."

Softly she said, "I know, Daniel, and it means a lot to me. Truly it does. I want you to know that."

He wondered if he should tell her he loved her. Or would it make her even more skittish than she was already?

"Heather misses you," she said, not knowing what he was thinking.

"I miss her, too. Is she over being mad at me?"

"She never has been one to hold a grudge. Of course she's over it."

An idea occurred to him. "When's her last day of school?"

"This Friday."

"Listen, you need time off to relax, and I want to spend more time with the two of you. How about the three of us take the weekend and go up into the mountains? We could leave first thing Saturday morning and come back on Monday."

"Monday? But I—"

He interrupted her argument, guessing what she was going to say. "You're the boss, Monica. You can take a day off if you want it."

"Oh, I don't know, Daniel. It's awfully short notice and I—"

He wasn't about to give up yet. "Sweetheart, I promised myself I was going to take advantage of the Idaho wilderness while I was home. Camping. Fishing. Hiking. The weather's supposed to stay unseasonably warm through the weekend. I've got all the equipment we would need right here in the basement. I can take the sleeping bags to the dry cleaners before five o'clock today, and we'll have them back by Friday. What d'you say?"

"It's been years since I went camping. I never was much of a Girl Scout."

He wished he was with her right now. He'd hold her in his arms and give her a long, slow kiss and help her make up her mind. "It's okay. I was a *very* good Boy

Scout. Always prepared, you know. I'll take care of you.''

Another hesitation, then, ''Promise?''

''Yeah. I promise.'' He wasn't talking about camping any longer.

He wondered if she knew that.

Chapter Ten

Monica didn't know if she was more nervous about her Friday night date with Daniel or the camping trip that weekend. It was easy to understand why she'd accepted his invitation for dinner and dancing, but she still couldn't figure out how he'd convinced her to take off for the mountains. She'd never been keen on roughing it, especially this early in the year when the Idaho nights could drop into the frigid thirties or lower.

She shivered just thinking about it.

Heather, on the other hand, was overjoyed by the planned excursion with her dad. She talked to him on the phone every night, and then she relayed the entire conversation to her mom. She packed and unpacked and packed again the things she thought she should take with her. Heather's excitement was so palpable, it was contagious. Even Monica began to wonder if the trip might turn out to be fun.

On Friday, she left work early and went to pick Heather up at school. She parked her minivan on the street and got out to wait on the sidewalk. The sun was warm and the sky was a perfect shade of blue. The air had a certain luscious smell of summer in it. She almost felt like a kid on the last day of school herself.

When the final bell of the school year rang, the kids poured out of the building, laughing and shouting, book bags and backpacks filled to overflowing. It took Heather only a moment to see her mother. She raised an arm and waved, then she shouted goodbyes to some friends and raced across the school parking lot. She arrived, panting and grinning.

"Summer!" she exclaimed, the single word completely expressing her jubilation.

Monica smiled as she gave her daughter a hug. "Summer," she echoed.

Still holding on to her mom around the waist, Heather looked up. "I told Mary we were going camping, and she was *real* jealous. She wanted me to ask her to come, too. I could tell. But I told her this was just for me and my dad. And you, too." She stepped away from Monica and tossed her bag into the minivan. "I wish it was tomorrow already."

"It will be before you know it."

They drove home, Heather keeping up a steady stream of talk about her friends and what their plans were for the summer break. Mary Stover was going to take riding lessons. Billy Parker was going to stay with his aunt and uncle in Canada for two whole months. The Wilson twins were going to Disneyland. Julie Kent's mom was expecting a baby in a couple of weeks, so Julie had been taking baby-sitting classes at the local Y.

When Monica's gentle questions brought Heather

around to talking about herself, it became quickly obvious the only thing that mattered to her this summer was spending time with her dad.

"Maybe I shouldn't go to scout camp," Heather said out of the blue, a frown furrowing her brow. "It'll be getting close to the time he's going back to Chicago. Maybe I should stay home and be with him more."

A tiny catch in her heart made it difficult for Monica to speak. "He wouldn't want you to change your plans, honey," she managed to say.

Heather glanced over just as Monica pulled the van into the driveway. "Do you think he might decide to stay in Boise? To live here?"

The dying of the engine seemed to mimic the feeling in her heart. "Your dad's got to return to his job, Heather. He's a very important man, and his work—" She stopped abruptly, finishing the sentence to herself alone. *And his work is more important to him than anything else. It always has been.*

Oh, how she wished it wasn't true.

Heather hopped out of the minivan, oblivious to her mother's disturbing thoughts.

Maybe a summer of love will be enough.

Monica removed the key from the ignition and reached for the door handle.

Liar.

A summer wouldn't be enough any more than taking a lover would be enough. She still wanted it all—husband, family, home, a lifetime together, happily ever after—but she couldn't see an answer to the dilemma. She knew Daniel's drive for success better than anyone. Once he was back in Chicago, in the thick of things, he would forget about Monica and Heather in Boise.

Don't borrow trouble for tomorrow. That was the advice her mother had always given. Monica decided it would be good advice to follow at the moment. Her heart would be no more and no less broken if she loved Daniel through the summer than if she tried to end it now.

"Mama? You coming?"

She nodded, hoping Heather could see her. She couldn't be sure since she was suddenly blinded by tears.

Daniel whistled an old Rolling Stones tune as he smoothed his hair with the brush one last time. Then he stepped back and surveyed himself in the mirror.

He was wearing his favorite Armani suit. Charcoal-colored with the finest of pinstripes. He always felt like a winner when he wore this suit, as if he could conquer the world. Tonight was more important than that. Tonight he wanted to conquer Monica's heart.

It hadn't been easy, settling for phone calls this past week, but he'd made himself do it. He'd hoped some absence might make her heart grow fonder. And he thought his plan had succeeded, at least a little. The flowers hadn't hurt his cause, either. Funny how good it had felt, sending that bouquet to her.

Whistling once again, he grabbed his wallet off the dresser and headed for the one-car garage attached to the house.

It took a lot of self-control not to speed across town, but somehow he managed it. The reservation he'd made at one of Boise's toniest restaurants wasn't for another hour, so he had plenty of time to pick up Monica and drive back downtown.

A quick glance to his right confirmed that the corsage was still on the passenger seat beside him. He'd given the florist precise instructions about it—a single, pale pink calla lily with a sprig of baby's breath and a white ribbon. The woman had done a good job of recreating the corsage Daniel had given Monica all those years ago.

It's been years since a man sent me flowers.

He felt an unexpected sadness as those words repeated in his mind. After all, he was partially responsible. She'd had a daughter to raise. *His* daughter. A lot of men didn't want to take on the responsibility of a stepchild, so they avoided single mothers.

"Idiots," he muttered.

Any guy with a brain would count himself lucky if he could win her heart.

Daniel hoped beyond hope that his own luck would hold.

A short while later, Daniel strode up the walk toward Monica's front door, his stomach tied in knots. He felt like a high school kid on his first date without a chaperone. Even his palms were sweaty.

His nerves didn't calm down any when Monica opened the door a few moments after he'd rung the doorbell. She was so beautiful, it nearly knocked him off his feet.

She wore a dusty rose slip dress that flattered every curve, falling gracefully into waves of fabric that stopped just above her knees. Her necklace was a simple heart-shaped pendant made from Black Hills gold. Matching earrings dangled from her earlobes.

"Wow!"

Her smile was shy.

"Wow," he said again, almost reverently this time.

"You said that already."

"I meant it." He held out the corsage. "For you."

"Oh, Daniel."

He thought there might be a shimmer of tears in her eyes as she took the clear plastic box from him.

"You remembered," she whispered. "It looks just the same."

He remembered lots more than just the calla lilies. He remembered the way she'd looked in the morning, with the sunlight streaming through their bedroom window, reflecting in her golden hair. He remembered the soft purring sounds she used to make in her throat as he'd traced his fingertips up her spine. He remembered the way she used to run across the campus to meet him for a few moments between classes. He remembered sitting in front of a blazing fire and listening as she shared her dreams, her hopes, her heart.

He remembered...

She kissed him on the cheek. "Thank you."

It was just a feathery light kiss, but it caused desire to surge through him. He longed to pull her close and kiss her in return, thoroughly kiss her.

"Hi, Daddy."

He didn't know whether to be glad Heather had chosen this moment to show herself or not. He cleared his throat, then smiled as he looked toward his daughter. "Hi, yourself."

"Gee, you look handsome."

"Thanks. You look good yourself. Got a hug for your old man? I've missed you."

Heather raced forward and threw herself into his embrace. "I'm really sorry I was so nasty to you after dance class last week. I shouldn't've been."

"And I'm sorry I didn't handle things better. I shouldn't have threatened to spank you. I wouldn't, you know." He leaned down to eye level with her. "I told you I was going to have to learn this father stuff. Forgiven?''

She nodded. Then she whispered in his ear, ''I'm glad you're taking Mama out.''

''Me, too,'' he whispered in return. He straightened. ''You ready?'' he asked Monica.

''Mother should be here any moment. Then we can leave.''

Once again, he looked down at Heather. ''Are you all packed and ready to go camping?''

''I sure am. Want to see my stuff?'' She grabbed his hand. ''Come on. You can tell me if I'm missing anything.'' She tugged him toward the stairs.

Daniel glanced at Monica.

''Go on,'' she said with a wave of her hand. ''I'll call you when Mother gets here.''

The lighting in the *Restaurant Magnifique* was muted, making the dining room seem intimate even though it was filled to capacity. Five minutes after their reservation time, Monica and Daniel were taken to a secluded table in a far corner.

The maître d' pulled out a chair for Monica and, after she was seated, handed her a menu. ''Your waiter will be Robert.'' He spoke with a thick French accent. ''He will be with you shortly. I hope you enjoy your meal.''

''Thank you,'' Monica replied, trying not to gawk at her surroundings.

A candle flickered in the middle of the table, its light reflected in the crystal wine goblets, the gold-rimmed china plates and the silver table service. The carpet was thick and lush underfoot. The linen tablecloths were a brilliant white as were the napkins in their ornate silver rings. Enormous original oil paintings decorated the walls, the pictures depicting what appeared to be Paris street scenes from the 1800's—women in bustled gowns and men in top hats and hansom cabs pulled by sleek horses. In another corner, a formally attired young woman played familiar love songs on a grand piano.

"This place is incredible," she told Daniel in a hushed voice. "I'd heard it was fancy, but this is beyond anything I'd imagined."

"You've never eaten here before?"

She sent him an amused smile. "I'm a single mom. We're more familiar with fast food."

But as she looked at Daniel, she thought how perfectly he fit into this elegant environment. He probably ate in restaurants like this all the time in Chicago. He probably didn't even pay attention to the prices listed in the menus.

She knew so little about the world he lived in, she realized. Her life-style must be very simple in comparison. Yes, she'd enjoyed her own brand of success, but she still lived quite the ordinary, middle-class life. She owned a home with a sizable mortgage, drove a three-year-old minivan, had an active, school-aged daughter and cleaned up after a dog of unknown breed who liked to dig in her flower beds and bury dog biscuits in the middle of the lawn. Daniel drove bright red convertibles, not minivans.

"Hey, why so serious?" he asked, interrupting her musings.

She shook her head.

He leaned forward. "Well, whatever it is that's making you frown, forget it. This is your night to enjoy."

There was so much tenderness in his voice she couldn't help but respond to it. She smiled. "All right."

"Shall we start with escargot?"

"Snails?" She wrinkled her nose. "I've never eaten them before."

He arched an eyebrow. "Thirty-three years old and never had snails smothered in butter and garlic? Well, we'd better take care of that. It's an experience not to be missed."

Their waiter arrived at that moment. He introduced himself as Robert, welcomed them to the *Restaurant Magnifique,* then invited them to start their meal with an appetizer and beverage. Daniel ordered escargot and a bottle of wine.

"Wine always goes to my head," Monica said when they were alone again.

"I know."

She felt a rush of warmth as she recalled one night in particular when they'd shared a bottle of wine in front of a roaring fire, talking and laughing, kissing…and more. But it was the memory of the aftermath as she lay in Daniel's arms, firelight flickering over their bare skin, that made her feel flushed.

Huskily, sounding as if he'd just remembered the same night, he said, "Have I told you how lovely you look tonight?"

She nodded.

"Then I'm telling you again, because you should hear it often. Monica, you're beautiful."

She didn't know how to respond. She was out of practice, she supposed. She wasn't used to getting this kind of compliment from a man any more than she was used to eating in a restaurant like this one.

She turned her gaze away from him, looking across the dining room toward the pianist at the grand piano. "She's very good, isn't she?" Monica closed her eyes. "Olivia Newton-John. 'I Honestly Love You.'"

"I honestly love you."

Her heart leapt at the way he repeated the song's title. It almost sounded as if...

She opened her eyes and met his gaze. Her breath caught in her chest, and she thought surely the people at neighboring tables would be able to hear the rapid pounding of her heart.

Was it possible he felt the same thing she did? Was it possible he'd meant those words as they'd sounded?

Robert's return broke their locked gazes. While the waiter poured a small amount of wine into Daniel's wineglass, Monica tried to still her racing pulse by taking deep, slow breaths. After sampling the wine, Daniel nodded his approval.

Robert filled both crystal goblets, then said, "Your appetizers will be out in a few more minutes."

"Thank you." Daniel's gaze returned to Monica. He lifted his glass toward her in a salute. "To summer...and beyond."

There went her heart again, slamming against her ribs, making it difficult to breathe, making it difficult to think clearly. She raised her goblet. "To summer...and beyond," she echoed him, then took a sip of wine.

Everything became a sort of blur after that. Perhaps it was the wine going to her head as usual. Or perhaps it was the way Daniel watched her, with tenderness and desire swirling in the depths of his silvery gray eyes. Or perhaps it was her own traitorous heart, a heart that loved him despite common sense, despite all the reasons it shouldn't.

Or perhaps it was a combination of all those things.

The dance floor was crowded with couples when Daniel and Monica entered the restaurant lounge two hours later.

They had lingered over their supper, making every moment an experience. They had talked of nothing important, and yet Daniel had been aware that underlying every word was a connection between them. He only had to look into Monica's eyes to know she was feeling the same connection.

They'd no more than sat down at a table in the lounge when the three-piece ensemble began to play a slow song. It was the only kind Daniel was interested in dancing to tonight. He wanted an excuse to hold her in his arms.

"Shall we?"

She nodded and allowed him to lead her by the hand toward the dance floor. Once there, he pulled her close to him, his right hand in the small of her back. They fit together, moved together, naturally. As if they'd been dancing together all of their lives.

Daniel could smell the fresh fragrance of her shampoo as he pressed his cheek against the side of her head. He could feel her heart beating near his own. His body responded to her closeness. He wished he could pull her even more tightly against him. He wished he could kiss her. He wished they were alone instead of surrounded by dozens of other couples. He wished he could remove that flimsy little number she was wearing and make love to her. He wanted her desperately.

They could go back to his place. No one would disturb them there. No Ellen Fletcher to disapprove. No Heather to stumble in on her parents accidentally. Just the two of them amid mussed sheets, their bodies fitting together even more perfectly than they were right now.

He couldn't remember the last time his blood had run

this hot in his veins. He couldn't remember the last time he'd ached for a women this way, the last time he'd yearned to see and touch and caress, to kiss and taste and become lost in another. He wanted to tell her a million times how beautiful she was. He wanted to show her with his body how much he loved her. He wanted to see her face as ecstasy flooded through her. He wanted to hear her cry out in pleasure.

"Daniel?" Her voice was muffled against his shoulder.

"Hmm?"

"Be careful with me."

The simple request nearly broke his heart, and he knew he couldn't take her to his place.

"I will, Monica," he whispered in her ear. "I promise."

Chapter Eleven

Monica slept very little that night. The bed seemed cold and much too large. She kept remembering the feel of Daniel's arms around her as they'd danced. It had been more wonderful than she'd imagined it would be.

It had also been more dangerous than she'd expected.

Be careful with me, she had pleaded, knowing her heart could so easily be broken now that she loved him again.

And Daniel had answered, *I will, Monica. I promise.*

She wanted desperately to believe him. She wanted to believe they had a future together as a family. But how? Even if he wanted marriage, his job was in Chicago and hers was here in Boise. She realized there were couples who had long-distance marriages, but Monica didn't want to be one of them. Could she leave her home, her parents, her friends and her business if Daniel asked her to? And if she couldn't, wouldn't it be wiser to call things off now?

By the time wispy clouds in the eastern sky were tinged pink by dawn's first light, Monica was wondering about the wisdom of spending a weekend with Daniel. Maybe she was only setting herself up for more heartache. Yes, she had promised to give him the summer. But what did that mean, after all? What did he want from her? Or did he even know?

With a groan, she cast off the blanket and sheet and got out of bed. She was tired of so many questions that didn't seem to have answers. She'd go mad if she kept thinking about it.

She showered, then dried her hair and put it up in a ponytail. She didn't bother with makeup except for some mascara.

A short while later, wearing khaki shorts, a cotton shirt and new hiking boots, purchased especially for this weekend, she went to Heather's room to wake her. She was already too late; her daughter was up and dressed.

"Is Daddy here yet?" she asked the moment Monica opened her door. Her eyes sparkled in anticipation.

"Not yet. We'd better eat breakfast so we'll be ready when he arrives."

"Should I carry this stuff downstairs first?"

Monica smiled. "Okay. I'll help you."

Heather led the way, lugging her duffel bag with one hand and carrying a pillow tucked under her other arm. "Daddy said he's gonna teach me how to fish. And if I catch anything, he says we'll eat it for dinner. D'ya think I'll catch a fish, Mama?"

"I don't know, honey. You might."

"I sure hope so. Mary said her dad's never taken her camping or fishing. She said she's gonna ask him to, next time she goes for a visit with him and her step-mom.''

Heather couldn't have any idea how her words affected Monica. If she and Daniel didn't make things work between them, then Heather would be shuffled between them for visits, just as Mary was between her divorced parents. Monica had been willing to accept that possibility a few weeks ago. But now that she loved him, now that she knew how much he loved his daughter...

"You want some toast, Mama?" Heather asked as she headed for the kitchen.

With a catch in her heart, she answered, "Okay," even though she wasn't the least bit hungry.

Daniel drove Monica's minivan along Highway 55, following the churning Payette River. The water was high from spring runoff, and kayakers were out in force on this early summer Saturday to experience one of the top white-water rivers in the country.

About midway in their drive, Daniel stopped at one of the many turnouts along the two-lane highway. They got out of the van and stood on the ridge above the river so they could watch the men and women in wet suits who were braving the icy waters below. The river plowed over rocks and boulders, white foam splashing high in the air. Reflections of sunlight created multiple minirainbows above the brightly colored kayaks that skimmed, plunged, rolled and turned in the water. It was obvious these kayakers weren't novices. They knew exactly what they were doing. If they didn't, they wouldn't have a prayer.

Monica and Heather both squealed as a kayak turned upside down immediately below them. A second later, it was uprighted by the kayaker's oar. The man grinned at Monica as he spun his lightweight canoe to face up-river, then paddled against the flow of water, waiting for one of his colleagues.

Show-off, Daniel thought. He draped a proprietary arm around Monica and another around Heather.

"This is way cool!" Heather exclaimed, looking up at him.

"Yeah, it is," he replied. But he didn't mean watching the kayakers. He meant being with her and her mother. He glanced over at Monica and wondered if this would be the weekend he should tell her he loved her.

No, he decided. He needed to prove some things to her. He understood that. She cared about him. She might even love him. But she was scared. She had no reason to trust him yet with the things that were most important to her. He had to show her he was a man who could be trusted, and he would have to do it carefully. If he rushed her, he might lose her for good.

"Well, campers," he said with a determinedly cheerful voice, "let's move along. I'd like to get camp set up before noon."

The remainder of the drive to Ponderosa State Park, a campground on the banks of Payette Lake, went swiftly. Heather taught her parents several songs she'd learned the previous year at Girl Scout camp, and the three of them sung them with varying degrees of skill. They often ended a verse with gales of laughter over their own performance. When singing got old, they played the alphabet game, searching roadside signs for words that began with each of the twenty-six letters of the alphabet. The trick, of course, was finding them in order.

It was past ten-thirty when the merry campers arrived at the state park. Daniel went into the ranger station to register them for a campsite while Monica and Heather used the ladies' rest room. By eleven o'clock, they'd found their site, a spot on a knoll overlooking the lake.

"Can I go down and see the beach?" Heather asked, glancing from one parent to another. "Just for a minute?"

"Sure," Daniel answered. "But stay where we can see you."

Heather darted off with Cotton galloping after her.

"Daniel, she should have helped us set up camp before she got to play."

He looked over his shoulder, meeting Monica's gaze. It was obvious she wasn't happy with the decision he'd made. "It couldn't hurt for a few minutes, could it? She's been cooped up in the car for a couple of hours."

"So have we."

"Then maybe you and I should join her." He held out his hand. "Come on. Let's see how cold the water is."

Monica tried to maintain her scowl of disapproval but failed. Daniel was too hard to resist, especially when he smiled at her that way. She took hold of his hand and allowed him to pull her down the path to the swimming area.

Heather had made her way to a deserted stretch of beach, away from the dock and those who were soaking up the early summer sun while seated on short-legged chairs or lying on oversize beach towels. She threw a piece of driftwood for the dog and laughed as Cotton chased it, tossing sand and water in every direction with her big paws.

Daniel's grip tightened on Monica's hand. "Thanks."

She looked over at him, but he was watching Heather.

"Thanks for not getting an abortion or giving her up

for adoption. I know you could have. I know it might have been easier." His voice was thick with emotion. "Thanks for letting me be her father."

Wordlessly she squeezed his hand in return. A wave of hope washed over her in that instant.

Maybe...

Just maybe...

Daniel cleared his throat, then called to Heather, "How cold's the water?"

"Like ice."

"Still want to go swimming later?"

"You bet!"

He chuckled and softly said, "Kids don't feel the cold like we do, do they?" He didn't wait for Monica to answer before calling to Heather, "Come on, squirt. We've got a tent to put up, and I need your help."

"Okay, Daddy. Cotton. Come here, girl. Let's go."

It didn't take Heather long to race up the trail and whizz right past her parents, her dog at her heels as usual. Daniel draped an arm over Monica's shoulders, and the two of them proceeded more slowly toward their campsite.

They must look like a real family, Monica thought, and that fluttering, butterfly-wings feeling filled her stomach once again.

The setting up of the tent was an occasion none of them would soon forget.

The canvas tent was old, and the instructions had long since disappeared. Daniel had thought he would remember exactly which pole went in what loop. It was soon obvious he'd been mistaken.

The third time the tent collapsed, this time with Daniel trapped inside, Heather was felled by the giggles. Monica laughed so hard she had to sit down. Their amusement only grew worse when Daniel finally poked his head out of the tent.

Gasping for breath and trying not to laugh himself, he pretended an offense he didn't feel. "You sure know how to hurt a guy. Making fun of him when he's down. There's only so much the male ego can take."

"Poor baby," Monica replied with an amused shake of her head, tears running down her cheeks.

He lifted one eyebrow. "You'll think 'poor baby' when you have to sleep on the ground under the stars instead of inside the tent. It *could* rain on you, you know."

"McCall has several nice hotels," she countered, unfazed by his threat.

Daniel cast a horrified look in Heather's direction. "A hotel? Are we going to stay in a *hotel?*"

"No!" his daughter exclaimed, then started giggling again.

"I should think not." He grunted. He muttered something else about a man's pride as he returned to work on the tent.

Somehow he and Heather straightened out the poles and ropes and stakes. At long last, their canvas abode rose victoriously from the forest floor—and remained standing.

Puffing out his chest, Daniel turned toward Monica who was, by this time, preparing a lunch of sandwiches made with cold cuts and cheese. "There," he said. "I told you we could do it."

She put down the knife she'd been using to spread mustard and applauded them. "Very good, Mr. Rourke. Most impressive. And you, too, Heather."

"You mock us, Ms. Fletcher. I can tell. Be careful,"

he warned, "or you just might find yourself taking a dunking in the lake."

"You wouldn't dare!"

He chuckled ominously. "Wouldn't I?" He moved toward her with deliberate, threatening steps. "Push me just a little more and see what happens."

"Stop right there." Monica picked up the knife again and waved it in his direction. "Or I'll add sweet pickles to your potato salad."

He grinned. She'd remembered he didn't like pickles in his potato salad. All these years, and she'd remembered a little thing like that.

He raised his hands in a show of surrender. "Truce?"

She smiled back at him. "Truce."

"I think for a truce to be binding it has to be sealed with a kiss."

Monica glanced toward Heather.

"Go on and kiss him, Mama."

Daniel advanced. Monica put down the knife.

He took hold of her upper arms and drew her toward him. She allowed her head to drop back as she rose on tiptoe.

He stopped smiling. So did she.

He kissed her. She kissed him back.

They belonged together, he thought as he tasted the sweetness of her mouth.

He knew it, and so did she.

Lost in his own thoughts, Daniel drove the minivan north along a dirt road.

It had been about nineteen years since he'd come with his dad to this fishing spot on the river that joined the upper and lower Payette Lakes. Daniel didn't have many good memories about his father, but the few he had were almost all tied to fishing. Richard Rourke had first brought his son to this spot when Daniel was about six or seven years old. He remembered catching a big trout that day, and he remembered the way his dad had slapped him on the back and praised him for a job well-done.

He glanced over at Heather. She was staring out the window with an eager expression on her pretty face. His heart slammed against his ribs, driven there by a feeling of love so strong it knocked the breath right out of him.

Watching the road ahead of him once again, he couldn't help marveling over all that had happened to him in the past few weeks. From a work-obsessed bachelor in Chicago to a dad on an Idaho fishing trip with his ten-year-old daughter. Who would have believed it? And who would have believed he'd feel this way about it?

"Mom should've come with us," Heather said, interrupting his thoughts. "She wasn't gonna do anything but read a book. She'd've had more fun with us."

"I'm not so sure." He chuckled. "I think she was glad to see us go so she could just relax in that lounge chair. I'll bet she's already taking a nap."

"This is gonna be more fun."

"Yeah, she doesn't know what she's missing."

It wasn't long before Daniel spied his turnoff. The van bumped its way over a narrow track of road, tall brush and trees shading the way before them. He was just beginning to wonder if he'd taken a wrong turn when the road opened up before him into a small meadow. This was it. The old fishing spot. And luckily, no one else had beat them to it.

"We're here," he said as he applied the brakes.

They had barely come to a halt before Heather unbuckled her seat belt and was out of the van. She opened the sliding door on the passenger side and began hauling out the fishing poles.

"Did you catch lots of fish here, Daddy, when you were a boy?"

Daniel lifted the tackle box with one hand. "I caught a few."

"I'm gonna catch a really big one, and then we're gonna fry it and have it for dinner."

"I hope so, squirt." He mussed her bangs. "I sure hope so." He rolled the door closed, locked the van, then picked up the tackle box and his fishing pole. "Let's go."

The sun was warm on his back as he followed a trail through tall brush and past stands of aspen. The song of the river, gurgling over smooth stones, serenaded them even while it was out of view.

He thought about his dad again, remembered the red flannel shirt Richard had always worn fishing and that ugly military green hat with fish hooks stuck in its crown. Tall and ruggedly handsome, Richard Rourke had loved the outdoors. He'd loved to hunt and fish, loved to escape into the wilderness.

The only times Daniel could remember the two of them being even remotely close had been up in the mountains on trips like this one. Maybe it was because they could just be two males playing the heap-big hunters. Maybe because his dad didn't have to act like a father out here but could just be a pal, and that's all he'd wanted to be to Daniel.

He didn't want Heather looking back someday and thinking, *That time we went fishing when I was ten was the best time I ever had with my dad.*

He wanted Heather to have so many "best times" she couldn't possibly remember them all.

Monica laid the book she was reading on her chest and stared up at the patch of sky she could see above the swaying ponderosa pines. She took a deep breath of clean, crisp air. How glad she was she'd agreed to come up here with Daniel. She could literally feel the tension draining out of her. Even if she tried, she couldn't have concentrated on the work awaiting her back at the office. And so she didn't try.

She closed her eyes, smiling as the memory of Daniel's most recent kiss flowed over her. Something special was happening between them. She'd sensed it in that moment. She'd felt some of her fear of the unknown dissipating. She'd felt herself beginning to trust him. Really trust him. She couldn't say why. She only knew it was true.

Her thoughts drifted to Heather. Her daughter was so happy being with Daniel. Monica used to think that Heather didn't miss having a father around, but she couldn't fool herself about that anymore. Heather would be heartbroken when he returned to Chicago.

She looked up at the sky again. "Chicago," she whispered.

She'd never wanted to live anywhere but Boise. She'd hated those months in Salt Lake City while she awaited Heather's arrival. And not just because of her situation. Salt Lake was too big, too strange. Boise was home.

Could she possibly be happy living in a city like Chicago? The winters were harsher there. The summers were hot and humid. There was the traffic, the crime, the crowds of people. And no mountains. Monica was an Idaho girl, a hometown girl. Boise represented everything safe and familiar and comfortable in her life. She didn't want to leave it.

But if she loved Daniel, really loved him, wouldn't that be enough to make her happy there? Shouldn't she be willing to make a sacrifice to be with him? Wasn't love enough?

Of course, he hadn't told her he loved her yet, let alone proposed marriage. She could be jumping the gun, even supposing. But if he did love her, if he did propose, wouldn't she be wise to know what her answer would be?

"Chicago," she said again, louder this time, then added, "and Daniel."

The two together didn't sound so bad.

They dined that evening on two rainbow and two brook trout. Heather took credit for three of the four fish, as well as for the largest catch of the day. Monica swore she'd never tasted anything better, and she meant it, too.

As dusk painted wispy clouds in shades of lavender, pink and peach, Daniel built up the campfire, and they all three roasted marshmallows on straightened wire hangers and made smores with graham crackers and chocolate bars. By the time brilliant stars twinkled against an inky black sky, Daniel, Monica and Heather had eaten their fill and begun singing camp songs in soft voices that blended together perfectly.

With the heat of the fire on her face and the glow of happiness in her heart, Monica didn't feel the evening's chill. She felt warm and wonderful. Even more so when Daniel unexpectedly took her hand in his, squeezing it gently.

Heather's eyes began to droop, despite her efforts to stay awake as long as her parents were up. Finally she gave in to her exhaustion. Monica went into the tent with her daughter, helping her to undress and put on a warm nightshirt. Heather was asleep within seconds of zipping closed her sleeping bag.

After Monica returned to the campfire, now burned down to glowing red coals, she and Daniel sat together, once again holding hands. Neither of them spoke. It seemed enough tonight to simply be together. Their silence wasn't strained; it was comfortable.

Around them, they could hear the sounds of other campers. Closing of trailer doors. A mother's soft words to a child. The bark of a dog, followed by a reprimand from its owner. Little by little, even these sounds faded away, until it seemed only Monica and Daniel remained in the forest.

She lay her head against his shoulder. He put his arm around her back. He brushed his lips across the crown of her head. It caused her heart to flutter, her breath to catch.

She closed her eyes, giving herself over to her senses. She heard the lapping of the lake upon its shores. She smelled wood smoke in Daniel's wool jacket. She felt the night breeze upon her cheeks, cool and fresh compared to the warmth of Daniel's body beside her.

Daniel's body beside her...

She opened her eyes, lifted her head, turned her face toward him. He stared back at her, the moment intense and filled with longing. She didn't need to ask him what he was feeling or what he was thinking. She knew.

She knew because she was feeling and thinking the same things herself.

It was a long, tortuous night for Daniel.

Lying right next to Monica, both of them zipped up

tight in their own separate sleeping bag, he'd felt every stone, every bump in the earth. He'd also heard every little sound Monica made, from her steady breathing to an occasional small sigh. He'd longed to hear her sighing for other, more intimate reasons.

It wasn't until the wee hours of the morning that Daniel finally fell asleep. His dreams delivered what reality had not. He dreamed of making love to her...slow, sweet, wonderful love.

When he awakened, Monica was snuggled close to him, her back to his chest, his arm wrapped around her. Smiling sleepily, he buried his face in her tousled hair. She moaned and scooted even closer against him.

He wanted to moan, too, but for a different reason. There was no hope of assuaging this burning desire at the moment. Not with his daughter sleeping just the other side of Monica. Not when Monica had made it clear she was not in the market for a lover.

His mouth went dry. His heart began to race.

Do it! his mind shouted.

What if she refused him?

Do it!

What if it was too soon?

Don't be an idiot. Do it now!

He lifted his head, brushed her hair away from her ear, then gently nibbled on the tender lobe before whispering, ''Marry me, Monica.''

He heard her tiny gasp. For a moment, even the earth seemed to be holding its breath. Then she rolled over to face him.

She stared at him. Uncertainty darkened her eyes. ''Are you sure, Daniel?'' She also spoke in a whisper. ''Really sure this is what you want?''

''I'm sure.''

"You thought you were sure once before. And then you changed your mind."

He didn't like being reminded of that particular part of his past, but he understood her lingering doubts. She'd spoken nothing but the truth.

"I won't change my mind," he said, hoping his voice would reveal how much he meant his promise. He'd never meant anything more. "I want you for my wife." His arm tightened. "I love you, Monica."

Tears slipped from the corners of her eyes. "I love you, too, Daniel. Maybe I've never stopped loving you."

"Then say yes."

"There are so many things to be considered."

He kissed her forehead. "None that can't be worked out." He kissed the tip of her nose. "None that matter." He kissed her on the mouth. "It only matters that we get married and be together. The three of us."

"We shouldn't rush."

He smiled. "We aren't rushing. It's already taken us over eleven years longer than it should have."

"Oh, Daniel." She hid her face against his chest.

"Say yes."

"But—"

"Say yes."

"What if—"

"Monica...say yes."

She looked at him again. Her eyes still glittered with unshed tears. A hesitant smile curved the corners of her mouth. "Yes."

He sealed her acquiescence with a kiss.

"When?" Heather asked immediately after her parents announced their decision. "When are you gonna get married?"

"I don't know," Monica answered. "We haven't even discussed it."

"Can I be your flower girl, Mama?"

"Well, if we have that sort of wedding, I suppose..." She cast a helpless glance in Daniel's direction.

"We've got lots of things to decide," he said to Heather. "But we'll include you as we make every single one of those decisions. Fair enough?"

Heather thought about it a moment, then answered, "Okay."

Monica smiled. Daniel's answer had been the perfect one.

"Are you gonna call Grandma and tell her? There's a phone at the ranger station. Can we go call her now?"

"Maybe we should tell her in person," Daniel suggested. He looked at Monica for confirmation.

She nodded. "I think that would be better."

Heather hopped up and down. "Can I at least call Mary? I can't wait till we go home. Can I, Mama? Can I?"

"Okay, but you have to wait until after breakfast. It's too early to call now."

"Mary's gonna be so surprised."

Monica nodded, thinking to herself that it wouldn't hurt to let Becky Stover know, via Mary, that Daniel was taken. She hadn't forgotten the way the divorced Mrs. Stover had come on to him the night of the school carnival.

She almost laughed when she recognized what she was feeling: jealous and possessive.

"What's funny?" Daniel asked softly.

She met his gaze. "Nothing," she answered with a smile and a shake of her head. "Nothing at all."

She opened the camp stove and lit the burners, feeling

surprisingly hungry all of a sudden. She rarely ate much in the morning, but that wasn't going to be true today. She lay strips of bacon in a skillet to fry, then whipped up some pancake batter. In a matter of minutes, the air was filled with delicious odors that made all of their stomachs rumble in anticipation.

While Monica flipped pancakes, Heather filled paper cups with orange juice and set out paper plates and plastic dinnerware on the picnic table, and Daniel started another campfire.

All of a sudden, Heather asked, "So does this mean my last name will change to Rourke?"

Monica paused with the spatula poised above the skillet. Heather's question made her realize anew that everything was going to change because of her decision to marry Daniel. Nothing was going to stay the same. Her home. Her business. Even her daughter's and her own last name. Everything was going to change.

It was scary and exciting at the same time.

She heard Daniel say, "That would make me mighty proud, to have you using my name."

"Can I tell Mary to call me that from now on?"

"It's okay with me. Monica?"

She turned around. "If that's what you want, honey," she answered Heather. When she looked at Daniel, she added, "I plan to use it myself."

Chapter Twelve

The remainder of their stay in McCall was just about perfect.

On Sunday, after Heather called Mary with the news of her mom's engagement, the family took a hike along the nature trails. They rented a speedboat and toured the entire lake, looking at the many beautiful cabins that lined the shores, some of them brand-new, some of them sixty years old or more. They went into McCall, the small resort town nestled on the south end of the lake. They perused the tourist shops, then ate dinner at a little Italian restaurant that featured delicious spaghetti and meatballs. Finally, they drove twelve miles to the hot springs outside of New Meadows and went swimming.

That night, Monica nestled close to Daniel—each of them in their own sleeping bag—and placed her head on his shoulder. They kissed and whispered sweet words of love to each other long after Heather had fallen asleep.

Oddly enough, they didn't discuss any of the decisions still to be made. This was a time for simply basking in the love they had found and lost, then found again.

Monday morning, they took their time breaking camp. They ate breakfast first, then they each rolled up their sleeping bags before dismantling the tent—a job much easier, but less hilarious, than the original assembly had been. After that, Heather threw a stick for Cotton while her mom washed the two skillets and few utensils and her dad started packing the back of the minivan. They were ready to leave by eleven.

Daniel noticed how quiet Monica was during the drive down to Boise, but he didn't try to force a dialogue. If something was troubling her, she would tell him when she was ready. They had settled the two most important things: they were in love, and they were getting married. Everything else would fall into place at the proper time.

Bless Heather's heart. As usual, she took up any slack in conversation. She let them all relive her experience of baiting her first hook with a nightcrawler and reeling in her first trout. She teased her dad about the fiasco of putting up the tent but tempered it with praise for how well it had stayed up for two nights. And she rhapsodized about the possibility of being a flower girl for her mom.

The more Daniel thought about it, the more he liked the idea of a formal wedding. Bridesmaids and ushers, flowers and candles, a seven-layer cake and champagne. The whole works. After all, he only intended to get married once so they might as well do it up right. Monica hadn't given any indication what her thoughts on this subject were, but between him and Heather, he figured they could convince her that a big church wedding was in order.

He grinned as he remembered Monica saying she planned to take the name Rourke after they were married. In this day and age, he wouldn't have been surprised if she'd kept her maiden name, but he was glad she didn't want to. It was probably just shy of medieval to feel the way he did. So call him a male chauvinist pig. He wanted his wife to be Mrs. Rourke.

Heather quieted, then fell asleep, about half an hour before they arrived at their destination.

As Daniel turned the minivan into Monica's subdivision, she glanced over at him and said, "I'd like you to go with Heather and me to tell my folks. We probably should do it tonight. As soon as Dad gets home from work. Is that okay?"

"Anytime you say."

"I'll call Mom when we get home."

"I wouldn't mind a shower and a shave before we go." He rubbed the stubble on his jaw. "You'd probably like that, too, before I decide it's time to kiss you again."

She smiled. That secret sort of woman's smile that made a fellow forget to breathe. "Yes, I think I *would* like that," she said, her voice husky. "You're welcome to use the guest shower instead of driving home, if you want."

Once the van was unloaded, Heather was given permission to go over to Mary's to play, and Monica gave herself permission to let everything else—the flashing light on the answering machine and the stack of unopened mail—wait while she took a shower. A few minutes later, she closed her eyes while a hot spray washed over her. Tiny surges of water massaged her scalp and skin. She reveled in the clean scent of the soap after two nights in a dusty campground.

As the bathroom filled with steam, Monica's thoughts drifted to Daniel, as was so often the case.

Married. She was going to marry Daniel.

It didn't seem real to her yet. It probably wouldn't feel real to her until they stood before the minister and he pronounced them man and wife.

Were they doing the right thing? Daniel had been back less than a month. Was she crazy to think she was in love with him again? Was he crazy to think he was in love with her? Was it only nostalgia they were feeling and not a lasting love?

We aren't rushing. It's already taken us over eleven years longer than it should have.

She let out a deep breath as his words repeated in her head. She had nothing to fear. She *did* love him, and she wasn't about to let doubts and her own insecurities frighten her into thinking otherwise.

She smiled as she tipped her head back and rinsed the shampoo from her hair, memories of lying in Daniel's arms in that old tent drifting through her mind. He'd kissed her and kissed her and kissed her, way into the deep hours of the night. He'd whispered all those syrupy sweet nothings in her ear, making her giggle and tingle. She hadn't cuddled and cooed so much since she was a teenager, teetering on the brink of sexual discovery. Only, because she was a woman who had known a man—*this* man—in the most intimate fashion, she had also felt extraordinary frustration in addition to her pleasure.

A shiver of pure, unadulterated longing swept through her. It was almost as if he were with her in the shower.

It was almost as if she could feel his hands upon her highly sensitive flesh.

It would probably be wise for them to marry sooner rather than later, she thought as she shut off the water and reached for her towel.

Maybe it was crazy to deny them both some release. It wasn't as if they'd never been lovers. It wasn't as if she was a teenage virgin. This was the twentieth century. No one paid attention to those old-fashioned moral codes anymore, the ones her mother and dad had drummed into her as a teenager. No one would think less of her if she let Daniel move in with her now.

She stopped drying off with the towel and looked at herself in the mirror. The truth, she admitted, was that *she* would think less of herself if she gave in. Those moral codes she'd been raised with—the ones she'd scoffed at as a liberated college student—might seem old-fashioned to the rest of the world, but not to her. Not anymore. She meant what she'd said to Daniel. She didn't want a lover. She wanted a husband, a union, a happily ever after. She was willing to wait for that moment.

She shivered again as she remembered her own breathless response to his kisses.

No one said the wait was going to be easy.

When Monica went downstairs, she found Daniel on the telephone. His back was to her as she entered the kitchen.

"Charley," he said sternly, "we've been through this already. You're not going to see me until September."

He shook his head as he listened to whoever this Charley person was.

"Someone else will just have to cover that story.

You've got plenty of good reporters working for you. Send Raymond Zimms. He's been dying for the right opportunity."

It had to be his boss, Monica decided.

"Well, as a matter of fact, I do have something more interesting going on around here. I'm getting married."

"*What?*" shouted the voice on the other end of the line.

Daniel laughed. "Don't have a heart attack, Charley. People *do* get married, you know? Even guys like me."

Monica could still hear the man shouting but she couldn't make out what he was saying.

Daniel turned, saw her, shrugged his shoulders and grinned as he held the receiver away from his ear. Finally he interrupted his boss. "Gotta go. Send Raymond after that story, Charley. You won't be sorry." He dropped the receiver into its cradle, still grinning.

"I take it whoever that was isn't happy with you."

"Charley Cooper. Best dang editor in the country, in my not so humble opinion, and diehard bachelor if ever I knew one. And, no, he's not happy with me at the moment."

"I thought not."

He stepped toward her. "Trouble with Charley is, he's never met a woman like you to change his mind about marriage." He captured her in a close embrace.

She wrapped her arms around his waist. "It sounded like he wants you in Chicago now."

"He does. But he isn't going to get me." He brushed his lips lightly across hers. "Not until I can take you and Heather back with me."

She released a tiny sigh. "I guess we'd better talk about that, hadn't we?"

"Yeah." He kissed her again, more thoroughly this

time. When he finally withdrew his mouth, he said, "Set a date, Monica. I'll be there with bells on."

"I was thinking more along the lines of a tux."

He chuckled. "Whatever you want. I'm here to please."

It was darn near impossible to focus on what they needed to discuss when he was holding her this close. However, she could think of several things he could do that didn't require any discussion.

"You're blushing," he said in a low, suggestive voice.

"I am not," she argued, even though she could feel the heat in her cheeks.

He kissed her again, then whispered, "Oh, yes, my darling, you most certainly are. Now why is that?"

She placed her hands on his chest and gently put some distance between them. "Daniel, be serious. We do need to talk before we see my parents."

He gave her a hangdog expression. "All right. If you'd rather talk than kiss."

"Not hardly," she muttered as she turned away from him and led the way into the family room.

They sat side by side on the sofa. Daniel took hold of her hand, and she couldn't help smiling in response. She understood all too well the need to touch and be touched.

"Item number one?" he prompted, pretending to be all business even as his gaze slipped to her mouth.

"Well." She cleared her throat. "I suppose that would be the wedding date and deciding what sort of wedding we want."

"Soon. Very soon. And I want one with all the trimmings."

Monica could almost hear her mother's voice: *It takes time to plan a formal wedding, dear.* "Six weeks," she said to Daniel. "Six weeks from now, on Saturday if the church is available. That should be enough time to make the necessary arrangements." She hoped she was right about that.

"And Heather will get to be a flower girl," Daniel reminded her.

"She'd be terribly disappointed if she wasn't."

"Yeah, she would." He brushed stray wisps of hair away from her forehead. "And I'd be disappointed for her."

"All right. That's settled then."

He kissed her, deeply, thoroughly. He kissed her until she was left breathless by the encounter, her brain in a fog.

They weren't getting very far very fast.

"Next topic," he whispered, his lips brushing against hers. "The honeymoon."

She could feel herself blushing again as her imagination ran wild.

"Two weeks in Hawaii," he suggested.

"Two weeks? I've never been away from Heather that long."

"Okay, one week. But still in Hawaii. One week of walking on beaches and making love in the moonlight."

He kissed the curve of her neck, causing gooseflesh to rise along her left arm and down her left leg. Her eyelids fluttered closed and the most she could do was moan softly and nod.

"See," he said, "it isn't hard to decide what we want to do."

She gave her head a slight shake, then drew back from him as she tried to calm the pounding of her heart. "We need to be serious, Daniel."

"Monica love..." The look he gave her was hot enough to scald. "I'm definitely serious."

She frowned, determined to act responsibly. "What about *this* house? What about your *father's* house? Are we going to keep them? Rent them? Sell them? What about Solutions? What do I do with my business? Is there a chance we might come back to Boise one day? Where are we going to live in Chicago? Is your apartment big enough for a family or do we need to find a house? Are the schools good where you live or will we need to think about a private school for Heather? Daniel, we have to talk about these things."

Her little speech had been as much for her as for Daniel. It seemed to do the trick.

He sighed, then leaned back on the couch. "You're right. I'll behave myself. But I'm not sure I have answers to any of your questions."

"We don't have to know the answers right away," she countered. "We just have to identify the issues."

"You sound like a reporter."

"I doubt that."

"I love you, Monica. Have I told you that today?"

"You said you were going to behave."

"Sorry." He lifted his hands in a sign of defeat. Then he grinned. "Here goes. I'll rent out my dad's house again. We can wait awhile to decide what to do with your house. We might want to keep it as an investment. Solutions? Hmm. It seems to me you've got the personnel to run it even if you're not here. Maybe you ought to think about opening a branch office after you move to Chicago. Unless you want to stay home and be a full-time wife and mom. Which would be okay with me, too, if that's what you want to do. You've talked about having more kids. Maybe now's the time."

It surprised her that Daniel was the first to bring up the subject of more children.

"I wouldn't mind a brother or sister for Heather," he added. "Maybe a couple of them."

Her heart fluttered in response to the tenderness in his voice and to the words themselves. To be pregnant with Daniel's child again, only this time with him wanting the baby, with him being with her from the conception to the delivery, to see him holding his newborn child and walking the floor at two in the morning.

Daniel didn't seem to know what she was feeling. He just kept addressing each question she'd brought up moments before.

"Will we come back to Boise someday? I don't know, Monica. There's not the same sort of job opportunities for me here as there is back East or in the Midwest, but maybe I ought to be looking at doing something else. It was the need to get away from the rat race that brought me to Boise last month. Where will we live in Chicago? In my apartment. Yes, it's large enough for a family. At least for the present. Later we might want to buy a house. Schools? I haven't got a clue, but I can find out by making a phone call or two. Want me to do it now?" He moved as if to get up.

"No, Daniel." She stopped him with a hand on his arm. "You don't need to call anyone right now."

He leaned toward her, his expression earnest. "I'm not making light of any of this, you know. It's all important to me, too. I just think it'll take time to discover what's right for us as a couple and as a family. But as long as we go into this marriage knowing we're going to stick together through thick and thin—no divorce, no easy way out—then I'm convinced each one of us will be satisfied as we look for answers." His voice lowered a notch. "Agree with me?"

She nodded, never letting her gaze waver from his, her heart welling over with joy.

"I'm not going to make the same sort of mistakes my dad made."

"I know that."

"And I'm not ever going to run from commitment again. I promise you that, too."

"I believe you."

After a lengthy silence, he kissed her again, afterward saying, "Sorry. I just can't seem to stop myself from doing that."

"I'm glad." She smiled. "I won't want you to stop yourself very often."

When Monica called her mother, telling her she wanted to come over and bring Daniel with her, Ellen invited them for dinner. "Be here at six, dear. You know how your father likes to eat on time."

"Yes, Mom, I know. We'll be there."

After Monica was off the phone, Daniel returned a few more calls from the messages he'd picked up earlier. When he hung up from the last call, he told her he had to run an errand but would be back by five o'clock.

To be perfectly honest, she was a little hurt that he didn't invite her along with him. The house seemed too empty and quiet after he left.

On a whim, she decided to go into the office. She wanted to tell Doug Goodman the news of her engagement. She called the Stover residence and asked the sitter if Heather could stay over for a couple more hours. After receiving an affirmative response, she called Solutions, making certain Doug was in his office. He was.

"Do you want to speak to him, Ms. Fletcher?" the receptionist asked.

"No, Terri," she replied. "Just tell him I'm on my way down and not to leave until I get there."

"I'll do it, Ms. Fletcher. See you in a bit."

As she drove toward downtown Boise, Monica wondered if she was wrong to tell Doug before she told her own mother. But the truth was, she would burst if she didn't share her joy with somebody. She simply couldn't wait another three hours. And Doug was not only a dear friend but the person she would need to entrust Solutions to in the near future.

She doubted he would be surprised. He seemed to have figured out what would happen before Monica did. It must be that analytical accountant's brain of his, she thought as she pulled into her reserved parking space in the underground garage.

I'm going to marry Daniel. I'm going to marry Daniel.

It was like being nineteen again, the way those words made her feel. She hadn't known love would make her all googly-eyed, like a girl with her first crush. It totally destroyed her image of herself as a no-nonsense businesswoman.

She grinned as she entered the elevator.

I'm going to marry Daniel.

He was right. Love would carry them through whatever decisions they had to make.

All of a sudden, six weeks seemed more like an eternity. Maybe she should have said four weeks. Or three. Maybe only two.

Terri looked up from her desk as the elevator doors opened. "Hi, Ms. Fletcher. Gee, you look terrific. Your holiday must have been great."

"Yes, it was, Terri. Thanks."

She breezed on through the open glass doors and headed for Doug's office at the opposite end of the building from her own. She returned greetings to other staff members. She was aware of the silly grin she wore and their reactions to it, and that only made her smile broaden.

Doug was alone in his office. Monica stepped inside and closed the door behind her, then leaned against it. "Hi," she said. "I'm back."

It didn't take her friend more than a few seconds to know something important had happened over the weekend. "Spill, Fletch." He rose from his chair.

"Daniel proposed. We're getting married."

"Some weekend." He came over to her and gave her a hug. "I'm happy for you, Fletch. Real happy."

"Thanks." She had tears in her eyes, but they were tears of joy.

"So when's the date?" he asked as he took a step backward.

"Mid-July. We have to see when we can get the church."

He lifted an eyebrow. "Mid-July?" His voice was teasing. "In a hurry, huh?"

She nodded.

"Doing the whole wedding routine, I take it."

"Yes. Heather wants to be a flower girl."

"You're going to be a spectacular bride." His tone was tender, and for just a moment, he sounded somewhat wistful. Then he grinned and said, "So when do I get to meet this Mr. Rourke? I'm wounded, you know. You never brought him in to let me see if he passed muster."

She shrugged. "Guess I'm becoming a risk taker."

"Good for you, Fletch. It's about time."

* * *

Daniel suspected his future mother-in-law had already guessed why they'd come. And even though Ellen had given him her grudging approval the last time they'd seen each other, he still wasn't sure how she would feel about the news of her daughter's impending nuptials. He supposed it would be a mixed reaction, considering he would be taking both Monica and Heather away from Boise.

"Did you have a nice time in the mountains, dear?" Ellen asked as she hugged her daughter.

"We had a wonderful time, Mom." Monica grinned. "Bet you never thought you'd hear me say that."

"No, I didn't." Ellen turned toward her granddaughter who was standing beside Daniel, holding his hand. "And how about you, Heather?"

"It was really cool. I caught three fish, and I baited my own hook with *live* worms."

"Oh, my." Ellen's eyes widened appropriately.

Daniel gave Heather's hand a squeeze. He and Monica had made her promise to let them break the news. He could tell, by the way she was switching her weight from one foot to the other, that she was dying to blurt it out.

Ellen waved a hand toward the living room. "Well, go in and see your father while I check on dinner. He's taking a catnap in his recliner."

"Can I help in the kitchen, Mom?"

"No, I can manage just fine. Shoo. Go on with you."

Monica cast a surreptitious glance in Daniel's direction. He gave her a wink of encouragement, then followed her into the living room.

Wayne Fletcher must have heard them coming for he was just getting up from his chair as they entered the room. He gave his daughter a hug and returned her kiss on the cheek with one of his own. He listened for a few moments to his granddaughter's fishing tale, then he turned his attention to Daniel.

Daniel was surprised by the sudden dryness in his throat and the nervous feeling in his gut. "Good to see you again, Mr. Fletcher," he said as he held out his hand.

"Likewise." Wayne shook the proffered hand. "You'll have to tell me all about Chicago. You've made quite a name for yourself in the news world."

Daniel shrugged, not wanting to talk about his work.

He remembered the evening he'd come here with Monica to announce their previous engagement. He'd known her parents disapproved of him and Monica living together, and he'd known they were as much relieved as anything by their news. But he figured they'd also looked at the cocky, headstrong kid he'd been and wondered if he could make their daughter happy.

He wanted this time to be different. He might not need Wayne and Ellen Fletcher's permission, but he sure as heck wanted their approval.

He looked at Monica. She smiled, as if understanding his thoughts. He felt better immediately.

"I'm going to step into the kitchen to get Mom," she said. "You three sit down and talk. Heather, tell your grandpa more about our weekend. He'll love to hear about the setting up of the tent."

Daniel didn't know if he wanted to kiss her for getting Heather talking, thus freeing him of having to answer questions and make small talk, or to pinch her for having Heather tell about the tent fiasco. But it wasn't long before he was laughing right along with his daughter and Wayne, and he decided kissing his future bride was more in order.

Monica returned with her mother in tow just as Heather finished telling her story.

"The vegetables are going to boil over," Ellen protested, to no avail.

"This will only take a minute, Mom."

Monica let go of her mother's hand and went over to the couch where Daniel and Heather were sitting. He rose and put his arm around her back. The moment was here.

Daniel looked straight into Wayne's eyes. "Mr. Fletcher." He looked toward Ellen. "Mrs. Fletcher. I've asked your daughter to marry me." He dropped his gaze to Monica. "And she's done me the honor of saying yes."

She smiled, her entire face aglow. He felt just as she looked—as if nothing could ever go wrong again.

"And I'm gonna be Mama's flower girl," Heather piped up.

Before Daniel knew what was happening, he was being hugged and kissed by Ellen and his hand was being enthusiastically pumped by Wayne while he received several slaps on the back.

No one thought about dinner for a long time.

In the kitchen, the forgotten vegetables boiled over on the stove.

Later that evening, after Heather had reluctantly gone to bed, Monica and Daniel sat on the sofa, Monica nestled in the comfortable curve of Daniel's arm, her head resting against his chest.

They were content to sit in silence, simply enjoying being with each other, both of them lost in their private thoughts. Daniel slowly stroked his fingers over Monica's hair, and she listened to the beat of his heart beneath her ear.

After a long while, she said, "The folks were really glad for us."

"Seemed to be."

"Mom's probably making lists right now."

He chuckled. "No doubt."

"Maybe we should have eloped."

"Maybe." He kissed the top of her head. "But I'm glad we didn't. Even if it's just for Heather and your mom."

Monica smiled to herself, thinking how lucky she was. She wondered how many men would have considered the feelings of the bride's mother and daughter the way Daniel had.

"I've got something for you," he said after another lengthy silence.

She raised her head, looking up at him, her eyebrows arched in question.

He shifted on the couch and pulled his arm from around her shoulders. Then he reached into the pocket of his Levi's. She was aware of all this without taking her gaze from his.

He took hold of her left hand. "If you don't like it, we can get something else."

She looked down just as he slipped a diamond engagement ring onto her finger. "Oh!" The marquise-cut solitaire glittered brilliantly on a wide gold band. "Daniel," she whispered, "it's exquisite." She looked up at him. "This was the errand you had to run." It wasn't a question.

"Yeah." He placed his arm around her again. "I wanted to make sure everyone knew you were taken. Your neighbors. Everybody at your office. Even strangers on the street." He gave her a sheepish grin. "Archaic, huh?"

"No, it's not. It's sweet." She kissed him. "Very sweet."

She wondered if anyone on earth felt as happy as she did at this moment. Then she decided they couldn't possibly, for she was the only one with Daniel.

Chapter Thirteen

"You look exhausted," Doug said in his usual blunt style several days later. "Staying up late with Daniel?"

Monica leaned back in her office chair. "I wish." She sighed, then gave him a weary smile. "Mom's got me so busy with details for the wedding that Daniel and I hardly have a moment to ourselves."

Her mother was inexhaustible. Like a drill sergeant whipping her troops into order, Ellen made sure each and every detail of the wedding was seen to in its proper time. There were the invitations to select, order, address and mail. There was the wedding gown to choose, followed by the necessary alterations. There was the hall to rent for the reception that would follow the ceremony. Flowers for the church, a bridal bouquet and a cake to order. Decisions needed to be made, one right after the other.

More than one night Monica went to bed wishing she and Daniel had eloped.

"That's how it always works. So I hear." Doug motioned toward the files on her desk. "Why don't we go over this stuff later? You should go home and take a nap."

In a defeatist tone, she said, "Mom would find me."

He laughed, but nodded in sympathy.

She was silent for a short while, then sat forward, placing her forearms on her desk and clasping her hands. "Doug, I'm going to make you a partner in Solutions."

"What?"

She had clearly stunned him by her sudden announcement. His expression left no doubt about it.

"I've given this a lot of thought," she continued. "If you're going to be running the company after I move to Chicago, you ought to have a share in its future."

"But, Fletch, I don't have the kind of money needed to buy into it."

"I'm not asking you to buy in."

He frowned. "Listen, as your accountant, I can't very well approve of you just *giving* away partnerships."

"I'm not asking for your approval. But if that's how you feel, we can work out the financial aspects of a partnership later. Right now, I just want it known that you *are* my partner and that you have a new title. Vice president."

"I...I don't know what to say."

"I wouldn't do this if I didn't think it was best for Solutions. This isn't because you're such a good friend to me. It's because you're the best person for the job."

"I appreciate that."

"Then it's settled." She rose and held out her hand.

"Well..." He stood and took her hand. "Yes, I guess it is. Partner."

They shook on it, both of them grinning.

Daniel chose that moment to arrive, walking into the office unannounced. "Looks like I'm a bit late," he said as he approached Monica's desk. Then he offered his own handshake and congratulations. "Monica told me about her decision to make you a partner. I'm glad she'll have you looking out for the company. It'll be one less thing for her to worry about."

The two men had met the previous week. It hadn't taken Daniel long to figure out Doug Goodman cared a great deal for Monica. A great deal more than just the friendship she felt for him in return. He could have easily felt jealous, but instead, he'd found himself liking the guy.

Daniel leaned forward and gave Monica a kiss— mostly for Doug's benefit. So, okay, maybe he *was* just a bit jealous. Maybe he felt a need to stake his claim. So sue me, he thought.

To Monica, he said, "I came to steal my girl for lunch. Can she get away before her mother comes up with another crisis?"

"I think she can manage that." Monica's smile made his pulse race.

The intercom buzzed, then Terri's voice said, "Ms. Fletcher, your mother is on line four."

The three of them exchanged glances. The men burst out laughing. Monica didn't look as if she found it nearly as amusing as they did.

"Too late." Daniel tried to sound sympathetic but knew he'd failed.

"Foiled again," Doug added with a wicked grin.

Monica waved for them both to be quiet as she lifted

the receiver. "Hi, Mom... No, I haven't had a chance to call them yet... Yes, they all went out in Monday's mail... The *Herald*? No, I haven't sent it to them. I was waiting for... Yes, as a matter of fact, he's here with me now." She held the phone toward Daniel. "She wants to talk to you."

He gave her a horrified look and warded her off with crossed index fingers.

She punched him in the arm.

He took the phone, muffling his laughter. "Hello, Ellen. What can I do for you?"

"I was in the bridal shop today and they told me you hadn't been measured for your tux yet."

"No, ma'am, I haven't."

"Daniel, really. You mustn't put it off. Can you get in there this afternoon?"

"Actually I was thinking about taking Heather fishing on the river." It was sheer perverseness that caused him to tease her this way.

"Fishing?"

"Right after I take Monica to lunch."

"Daniel Rourke, the wedding is less than four weeks away. Even your best man has been fitted for his tux. Tony Cristobal went into the bridal shop the day after I talked to him, and he's certainly much busier than you are, what with his construction business and all. You really can't put this off another minute."

He could imagine his future mother-in-law flushed with frustration. Monica punched his arm again and glared at him, as if she'd read his mind.

"Okay, Ellen. I know this is important. I'll go in this afternoon and take care of it."

"Wonderful. Thank you, Daniel. Now, may I speak to Monica again?"

"Sure. Here she is." He passed the phone to her. "Back to you," he whispered.

A few minutes later, Monica placed the receiver in its cradle and met Daniel's gaze. "I'll be glad when this is all over."

"We both will."

"I haven't even begun to pack for the move." The strain was showing in her eyes. "I don't know what we'll need and what I should put in storage."

He took hold of her hand. "Come on. You need that lunch and some time without any demands. Get your purse."

"I really should stay—"

"Doug, tell your partner she has to go to lunch."

Doug nodded. "Go, Fletch. Daniel's right. Take a couple of hours and stop thinking about it all."

"Okay." She sighed. "Maybe you're both right."

Twenty minutes later, Daniel's car pulled up in front of his dad's house.

"I thought we were going to lunch," Monica said as he cut the engine.

"We are." He opened his door and got out, then came around to her side of the car. "Come on inside."

She raised an eyebrow but took hold of his hand and let him help her out. He didn't let go as he led her up the walk.

The moment Daniel opened the front door, Monica saw the small dining-room table was set with china and crystal, three unlit candles in the center. Sheer curtains at the living-room windows let in a soft light. The sweet strains of a Straus waltz drifted from the speakers of the CD player.

The door closed behind them. Suddenly Daniel's

hands were on her shoulders. He turned her to face him. "At last. I have you all to myself."

She stepped into his arms and indulged herself in the warm emotions surging through her as they kissed. She let herself forget the myriad problems and decisions and tasks that had filled her days the past few weeks. Instead she thought only of Daniel and the love they shared. Nothing else mattered at the moment.

He drew slightly back. "You make me forget why we came here." Desire made his voice deep.

"To eat." She sounded much the same.

"Oh... Yeah." He kissed her again, lightly this time. "Then I guess we'd better." With a hand in the small of her back, he guided her to the table, then pulled out a chair for her. "I'll be right back." He disappeared into the kitchen.

Monica looked at the beautiful table setting. Daniel had gone to a great deal of effort to make everything look so lovely. "Are you going to spoil me like this once we're married, Mr. Rourke?"

"I plan to, Ms. Fletcher," he replied from the other room.

She smiled to herself. It wouldn't be long before Ms. Fletcher was a name of the past and she became Mrs. Rourke. Monica Rourke. Mrs. Daniel Rourke. If she was sixteen again, she would be writing the new name across the covers of her notebooks, testing the way it looked on paper and crossing out letters to see if she and Daniel were meant for each other.

She heard his approach and looked up in time to see him step through the kitchen doorway, two plates in hand. And on those plates were diced wieners and baked beans.

Expecting an elegant meal to match the table setting,

Monica was momentarily stunned into silence. Then she started to laugh. She laughed so hard, tears ran down her cheeks.

"It's not *that* funny," he protested, but he couldn't disguise the twinkle in his eyes nor hide the grin that tweaked the corners of his mouth.

When she could catch her breath again, she said, "This was what I needed, Daniel. To laugh. It just might restore my sanity."

"Good." He kissed her forehead. "And just in case you've lost your taste for this particular delicacy, I've got tossed salads waiting in the kitchen. Mixed greens, baby tomatoes, onions and croutons with nonfat ranch dressing on the side."

"Just the way I like it."

"Just the way you like it."

The telephone interrupted their byplay. Daniel murmured something unintelligible as he went to answer it.

Monica dried her eyes with her napkin, still smiling. Wieners and beans with china and crystal. He'd known it would make her laugh. That was the whole reason he'd done it. No wonder she loved him.

"How bad is it?"

She wasn't sure if it was his tone of voice or the words themselves that caught her attention. She twisted in her chair.

Daniel stood in the doorway between the dining room and kitchen. He was frowning, his eyes worried. "Of course... Sure... I understand."

Her stomach tightened.

He met her gaze. "Okay, Charley. I'll do it... I'll call you as soon as I know when. Bye."

She stood as he hung up the phone.

"That was Charley Cooper."

"What's wrong?"

"Ed Tuskin, one of our reporters, was shot. They're not sure he'll make it."

"Oh, Daniel, I'm sorry. Was he a close friend of yours?"

"Close enough." His eyes searched hers for understanding. "Charley wants me back in Chicago as quick as I can get there. Ed was covering an important assignment, and Charley needs me to take over."

"He wants you *now?*"

He nodded.

"What about the wedding?"

He stepped forward and took hold of her shoulders. "I'll be back for the wedding. Nothing will keep me from it."

"I'll miss you horribly." She blinked at the rising tears.

She was being silly. She knew it. It wasn't all that long. Just a few weeks. She could stand a few weeks without him. It wasn't as if she hadn't been on her own for years. After the wedding, they would be together for the rest of their lives.

"Come with me, Monica."

Her eyes widened in surprise.

"You and Heather. Come with me."

"But there's so much—"

"Nothing your mother can't handle."

"But—"

He pulled her closer. His voice lowered. "Come with me. Call it a vacation. You could familiarize yourself with Chicago. You and Heather could see my apartment and decide what we need to make it more of a home." He paused, then added, "I don't want to be without you. Not even for three weeks."

"Mother will have a fit."

He kissed her.

"It would be such a crazy thing to do."

He kissed her again, then drew her into the circle of his arms.

"How can I—"

"Just for a couple of weeks." His breath was warm against her forehead. "Then you can come back to take care of all those last-minute things. Please go with me."

"I shouldn't. I know I shouldn't." She sighed. "All right, Daniel. We'll go with you." She drew back and looked at him. "But *you* have to tell Mom."

He smiled. "Done."

Daniel was able to book them on a direct flight to Chicago the next afternoon. Monica couldn't believe it happened so quickly.

Their seats were in the first-class cabin. Heather chose the window, and Monica sat next to her. Daniel was directly across the aisle from them.

Monica made certain her daughter's seat belt was fastened snugly around her waist, then did the same for herself. She retrieved a book and her reading glasses out of her purse. She took a swig from her water bottle. She tucked the soft airline blanket around her legs. She poked at her carry-on bag with the toe of her shoe, making sure it was properly stowed, according to the attendant's instructions. Then she checked Heather's seat belt a second time.

Monica didn't realize how tense she was until she heard Daniel say, "Relax, sweetheart."

The airplane began to taxi toward the runway.

She gave him a tight smile. "I'm not a very good flier," she confessed. She didn't bother to tell him she could count on one hand the number of trips she'd made by air, all of them many years ago.

The captain announced they were next in line for take-off and asked for the flight attendants to be seated. Monica gripped her armrests, all the while telling herself to relax.

The plane began to roll forward. Faster and faster and faster.

"Wow, Mama, look at that! This is way cool. We're off the ground."

She couldn't have looked to save her soul. Her eyes were squeezed shut. She even had to remind herself to breathe.

Yes, breathe. That would be a good idea. In… Out… In… Out…

"Mama, I can see our house. Look."

Monica opened her eyes a slit just as the airplane banked sharply to the right. Maybe she could have seen their house as she stared straight down at the ground, but it took all her concentration to keep from screaming.

As the plane leveled off, she squeezed her eyes shut again, mentally repeating lines from the Twenty-third Psalm. She skipped the part about the valley of the shadow of death. She was only vaguely aware of Daniel's hand covering hers on the armrest.

It seemed an eternity before the flight attendant's voice came over the speaker, saying passengers could get up and move around the cabin. Not on a bet, she thought.

"Why didn't you tell me?" Daniel asked, his voice deep with concern.

"I thought it might not be so bad," she answered hoarsely. "The last time I flew I was in my early twenties. I thought I would have outgrown it." She dared to open her eyes. He was hunkered down in the aisle beside her seat. She tried to smile at him. "Guess not, huh?"

"Want to listen to music? I've got some good CDs with me. Maybe it'll help."

Monica was willing to try anything at this point. She nodded. "Okay."

He slipped back into his seat and pulled his carry-on bag onto his lap. Meanwhile, the flight attendant serving the first-class cabin came down the aisle. She stopped at Monica's and Heather's row.

"Ms. Fletcher, would you and your daughter like a beverage?"

"My mom's scared," Heather volunteered.

The flight attendant, a pretty woman about Monica's own age, gave her a sympathetic look. "This isn't such a long flight, ma'am. We'll be on the ground before you know it."

"Have you been flying long?" Monica managed to ask.

She nodded. "Thirteen years. I promise you, it really is safe."

Monica forced a smile, but she suspected it was more of a grimace. "Thanks."

The woman looked at Heather. "Would you like something to drink?"

"I'll take an orange soda, please."

"And you, Ms. Fletcher?"

"Nothing for me, thank you."

The flight attendant nodded and moved to the next row. As soon as she was out of the way, Daniel reached across the aisle and handed Monica his CD player and a couple of CDs.

"I think we should reconsider our plans for a honeymoon in Hawaii." There wasn't any resentment in his suggestion. Only sympathy. "We can spend our wedding night in Boise, then drive over to the coast. It's only about eight hours to Portland."

Dear heaven! She hadn't even thought about the long flight to Hawaii. How many hours would they have been in the air, nearly all of it over the ocean?

She felt faint at the mere idea.

Something told her she wasn't cut out to be a jet-setter or even much of a business traveler. She was, and always would be, a hometown girl.

In a secret corner of her heart, she felt the first hint of homesickness.

A haze lingered over the Chicago skyline, tinged a pale lavender by the setting sun at their backs. The limousine headed east, one link in a giant chain of nonstop traffic on the John F. Kennedy Expressway leading from O'Hare International Airport.

Heather talked excitedly about everything she saw out the windows of the long, black automobile, but her mother didn't say a word. Daniel was glad to see color returning to Monica's cheeks, even though she was still abnormally quiet. He'd wondered more than once during the flight if she was going to pass out.

He squeezed her hand. "You okay?"

She nodded.

He didn't want to say anything to her now, but this put a definite damper on more than just an Hawaiian honeymoon. Daniel traveled frequently with his job, and he'd thought it would be great if Monica and Heather accompanied him some of the time. At least during the summer months when Heather was out of school. But if Monica was this afraid to fly, there was no way he would subject her to it. Which would mean they would be apart, sometimes for weeks at a stretch, when he was on assignment.

That reality didn't sit well with him.

Nearly an hour later, he unlocked the door to his apartment and ushered Monica and Heather inside.

"Wow!" his daughter exclaimed when she saw the wall of glass windows. They offered a spectacular view of twinkling lights as night began to blanket the city.

Daniel closed the door. "Are either of you hungry? We can order in for tonight, and tomorrow we'll stock up on groceries."

"I'm hungry!" Heather answered.

Monica shook her head. "I think all I want is to go to bed."

"Are you sure you're okay?" he asked her again.

"I'll be fine in the morning. Honest I will."

Daniel had an odd sensation in his gut, something telling him there was more wrong here than just a fear of flying. But for the life of him, he couldn't figure out what it was. Especially if she wouldn't talk to him.

"Why don't I order a pizza, then I'll show you both around the apartment? You can get settled in, make an early night of it and get a good night's sleep."

"Thanks," she whispered.

After placing the pizza order, Daniel gave them the tour of the place he'd called home for several years. In addition to the spacious living area, there was a large gourmet kitchen, with copper pots and pans hanging above the island stove. Off the master suite was an office with a computer and modem, fax machine, printer, copier, bookcases and file cabinets. It was tidy at the moment because he'd been away, but when he was working, the room always looked as if a tornado had blown through. Across the hall from the office were two smaller guest bedrooms, one on either side of a bathroom.

"I thought Heather might like this one for her room," Daniel said as he flipped on the light in the larger of the two bedrooms. Other than the double-size bed, a nightstand with lamp and a dresser, the room was empty, devoid of any personal touches. "It doesn't look like much now, but I figured you could decorate it like you want," he told his daughter.

"Whatever I want?"

"Sure. Your mom can take you shopping. Fix it up real nice so when we move back here after the wedding, it'll already feel like home."

Monica cast a surreptitious glance in Daniel's direction. Will it ever be like home? she wanted to ask him. She felt small and petty and spoiled. "And my room?"

He met her gaze, and she knew he wanted to ask her to share the master bedroom. To his credit, he didn't ask.

The second guest bedroom was as sparsely furnished as the other. Monica didn't care, as long as the bed was comfortable. She just wanted to sleep and forget the terror of their flight here.

The phone rang, and Daniel went to answer it. From down the hall, she heard his voice.

"I'd like to take the weekend to help Monica and Heather get familiar with the city. They haven't... Well, sure, I understand... No, if that's what you need, Charley... Okay, I'll be in by ten... All right. Good night."

By the time Daniel returned to her bedroom, Monica was unpacking her suitcase.

"I've got to go into the office tomorrow."

"I heard."

''Think you and Heather will be all right on your own for a few hours?''

She glanced over her shoulder and gave him a smile she didn't feel. ''Of course we'll be all right. It isn't like we're not used to being on our own.'' Just not in a strange city.

''Monica...'' He said her name softly, tenderly, as he turned her to face him. ''What's wrong?''

She fought unwanted tears. ''I don't know. It's silly really. I feel like such a child.''

He brushed his fingertips across her cheeks. ''Homesick?''

She nodded.

''It's not a crime to feel that way.'' He gathered her close against him. His hand stroked her hair. ''I love you, Monica. It'll be all right.''

She nodded again, but the heavy knot in her stomach wouldn't go away.

Chapter Fourteen

Monica awoke early the next morning, resolved to fall in love with Daniel's city. As long as she was with him, she could be happy anywhere. She loved him, and he loved her. That was more than enough to smooth over any rough edges associated with her relocation.

She took a shower, then dressed in a cotton blouse and skirt, remembering how warm it had been when they arrived yesterday. A comfortable pair of sandals completed her outfit. A final glance in the mirror told her she looked much better than when she'd gone to bed the night before.

As she walked down the hallway, she was surprised to hear the clatter of pots and pans coming from the kitchen. She'd thought she was the only one awake.

Daniel turned as she entered the room. For a moment, he assessed her appearance with his eyes. Apparently she'd been correct about looking better because he looked pleased. "You must have slept well."

"Yes, thanks."

He strode across the spacious kitchen and caught her up in his arms, kissing her tenderly. "In fact, you look more beautiful every time I see you," he said when their lips parted at long last.

She smiled in reply.

"I wish I didn't have to go into work today." His voice was husky. "I want to be with you."

She felt the same way.

"I love you, Monica."

"And I love you."

He kissed her again. A kiss that began gently but grew deeper and hotter with each passing second. Desire flared in her belly. July 18 seemed a long way off. She didn't know if she could stand the wait.

"Clickin' teeth and swappin' spit."

At the sound of the unexpected voice, they broke apart, both of them looking at their daughter who stood in the doorway.

"*What!*" Monica exclaimed. "Where on earth did you hear such an expression?"

"That's what Mary's grandma calls French kissing."

She wanted to ask where Heather had learned about French kissing but decided that was a silly question. Sex was used in television and magazine ads to sell everything from soup to nuts. Heather probably knew more now than Monica had when she was eighteen. It was not a comforting thought.

Daniel obviously didn't have the same concern. He grinned as he put his arm around Monica's shoulders. "You'd better get used to seeing me kissing your mom, squirt, 'cause I plan to do it as often as I can."

Heather wrinkled her nose and said, ''Gross,'' but she looked delighted despite her comment.

Daniel gave Monica one last kiss on the cheek, then went to the stove. ''I ran out early this morning for some groceries. Enough to see us through breakfast anyway. Do you like Cream of Wheat or oatmeal with raisins? I fixed both, just in case.''

Monica opted for Cream of Wheat. Heather asked for oatmeal. While Daniel filled bowls with the hot cereals, Monica poured herself a cup of coffee.

Before she could ask, Daniel offered, ''I got some of that nonfat French vanilla creamer you like. It's in the fridge on the top shelf.''

Her heart did a little skip. It was a small thing, remembering that she liked flavored cream in her coffee, yet it seemed a great deal to Monica. As an adult, as a woman, she'd never had anyone around to do things like that for her. Until now.

Her apprehensions of yesterday melted away, and she allowed herself to bask in thoughts of her sunny future with Daniel.

They ate breakfast in the kitchen eating nook, the three of them seated around a small glass-and-chrome table. Daniel apologized again for having to go into work their first day in Chicago, then made a few suggestions about what they might want to do while he was gone.

''Why don't you just get the lay of the land today. Familiarize yourself with the neighborhood. Maybe take a walk along the lakeshore. Tomorrow, we could go to Lincoln Park Zoo, if that's what Heather would like to do.''

''The zoo? That'd be cool, Dad!''

''Okay then, it's a date.'' He got up from the table

and carried his dishes to the sink. "I'd better go. Charley'll be waiting for me."

Monica followed him into the living room, then waited there while he went to his office to get his briefcase. A few moments later, he returned.

As he gave her a goodbye hug, he said, "Remember, you're not in Boise now. Take the usual big city precautions. Be aware of what's going on around you. That sort of thing."

She gave him an amused smile. "Boise isn't *that* small. I know what to do. We'll be careful."

"I'll be home as soon as I can." He kissed her cheek. "I'll miss you."

"We'll miss you, too."

The story was the hottest thing Daniel had seen since he was assigned to the Henderson investigation over three years ago. If Ed was correct—and it appeared he was—this could blow the lid off drug trafficking and other illegal activities in the entire state of Illinois and beyond to Washington. There were some names in the file one would never expect to see connected with heroin and cocaine and money laundering: state and federal government officials, law enforcement officers, entertainers, even a well-known clergyman.

"You can see why I wanted you back to cover this," Charley said after he'd given Daniel some time to glance through the thick file.

He looked up. "Was Ed shot because he got too close to the truth?"

"That's my personal feeling. But he was in a seedy part of town. It could be totally unrelated." By his tone of voice, it was apparent Charley didn't think it was remotely possible that the shooting was unrelated to the investigation.

Despite the potential danger, Daniel felt a spark of excitement. It was the sort of investigative reporting he thrived on. This was the kind of story that made people rush for their papers every morning.

Charley leaned forward in his chair. "We're close to cracking this thing wide-open, Rourke. Real close. We can't let this trail get cold now or it could all go down the drain."

"I know."

"So far, there haven't been any leaks that I'm aware of. If there is, we'll lose our edge. The television affiliates will be all over it, like maggots on a deer carcass."

"Is it possible for me to talk to Ed?"

The editor shook his head. "He's in a coma, although they're a little more optimistic he might survive. If he does, he could be paralyzed from the waist down."

Daniel felt sick at the news. Ed had a wife and two young kids. What was going to happen to Yvonne and the boys?

"I want you on this day and night until we've got everything we need to go with it."

"Remember I'm getting married the middle of July."

Charley barked a laugh. "If you don't have this wrapped up before then, Rourke, you're fired."

Daniel figured his boss was only half joking. This sort of coverage would generate incredible attention and accolades for the paper that broke it first.

He rose from his chair. "I'd better get to my office and read through this file thoroughly."

"Ed had some appointments made. See if you can't keep them in his place."

Daniel nodded. "I'll do it." Without another word,

he headed for his office, his mind already whirring with possibilities, angles to explore, interviews to conduct.

It was a picture perfect day. A breeze blew off the lake, chasing away the humid heat that had greeted them upon their arrival. The sun hung suspended in a clear blue sky. People were out in droves—jogging, walking their dogs, bicycling.

Heather drank in the sights with her usual enthusiasm, totally unfazed by the sheer size of the city and its population. She thought it was ''way cool'' that the city of Chicago had nearly three times the number of people as there were in the entire state of Idaho. Monica, on the other hand, felt like the proverbial hick from the sticks. She kept looking over her shoulder, just waiting for the mugger that was going to knock her down and steal her purse. Or worse.

By the time they returned to Daniel's high-rise apartment building, Heather had made a mental list of things she wanted to do during the next couple of weeks. High on the list, right after the zoo, was a Cubs baseball game and a visit to the Six Flags amusement park. Monica was just glad to be once again behind a locked door.

Coward, she chastised herself more than once. She felt totally out of her element and very unsophisticated. It was not a pleasant feeling.

She checked the answering machine for a message from Daniel. There was nothing from him, but there were two calls from her mother. She dialed the Fletcher residence, then began to unpack the groceries she and Heather had purchased on their way back to the apartment.

''Hello.''

''Hi, Mom.''

"Oh, Monica, dear. I'm so glad you called me back."
Ellen immediately launched into a litany of wedding details.

While she listened to her mother, Monica put a pan
of water on the stove, then opened the package of lasagna noodles so they would be handy when the water
came to a boil. Next she heated a large skillet in which
to brown the ground beef and sausages. Every so often
she made appropriate noises into the mouthpiece of the
telephone so Ellen would know she was listening. By
the time she hung up, the sauce was simmering over low
heat while the noodles drained on a towel.

She checked her watch. She'd expected Daniel to be
home by now. She wondered if he had Call Waiting on
this line. If not, maybe he'd tried to call her and couldn't
get through.

She turned on the oven so it would preheat, then went
to check on Heather. Her daughter was curled comfortably on the sofa, the television blaring.

"Dinner will be ready in about an hour," she announced.

"Great! I'm starving."

"What are you watching?"

"Same stuff that's on at home." Heather seemed surprised by that fact.

"It's cable TV. I guess everyone in the country has
basically the same channels these days." Monica looked
at her watch again.

As if reading her mother's mind, Heather said, "I
wonder what's keeping Daddy. Shouldn't he be home
by now?"

"I'm sure he'll be here soon."

Daniel leaned back in his chair and stretched his arms
over his head. His neck and shoulders ached, and his

eyes hurt from going through so many papers, reading line upon line of tiny print. But he hadn't been able to stop. Ed had put together an astounding amount of detailed information, some of it very damning. Daniel hadn't known Ed was this good. If he'd known...

He smiled half humorously. So this was what it was like to have some hotshot kid breathing down his neck. When Daniel had first come to Chicago, he'd always been waiting and watching for the chance to write a story that would catapult him into the top spot, right over the head of the paper's most respected reporter. A man Daniel had considered an old-timer ready for retirement. Now he wondered how often Ed had thought about him the same way.

His smile vanished. No matter what Daniel was able to do with this story, he was determined most of the credit would go to Ed Tuskin. He hoped Ed would be around to get the accolades for it. Even more important, he hoped the young father would be able to watch his sons grow up, hopefully play touch football or baseball or golf with them as they got older.

He turned to look out the window and was shocked to find evidence of dusk tinting the sky. Was it *that* late?

He reached for the phone and dialed his home number. Monica answered on the third ring. "Monica, I'm sorry," he said without giving her a chance to do more than say hello. "I got tied up at the office. I didn't realize what time it was."

"It's okay, Daniel. I knew it must be important. Although I *was* getting a little worried when I didn't hear from you."

He felt like a total jerk.

"I've kept your dinner warm. Heather was hungry so she and I ate quite some time ago."

Now he felt worse.

"She's anxious to tell you what we saw today."

"I'll be out the door in five minutes. See you soon."

He'd already hung up the phone and was shutting down his computer when Charley stopped by his office. "I thought you'd still be here, Rourke. Mighty interesting reading, isn't it?"

"Yes." He got up from his chair and reached for his briefcase.

"I've set up a meeting with Senator Neumeister tomorrow morning at nine. I want you to be there. We're meeting in his attorney's office." He handed Daniel a slip of paper. The law firm's name and address were written on it in Charley's bold script.

"Which way is Neumeister leaning?" Daniel asked. "Is he going to be honest or will he cover for his friends in the state senate?"

"I think he'll confirm most of Ed's information."

Daniel whistled softly.

"Meet me at that address at eight forty-five. I'll wait on the sidewalk, and we'll go in together."

"I'll be there."

They left Daniel's office and walked together toward the elevator, still talking about the particulars of the story.

It wasn't until Daniel was halfway home that he remembered he'd promised Heather he would take her to the zoo the next day.

Monica listened as Daniel explained to Heather why he would have to work on Saturday instead of taking her to the Lincoln Park Zoo. She saw the disappointment in their daughter's eyes even as she said, "It's okay, Daddy," and gave him a hug.

"How about Sunday?" he suggested.

"Okay."

He straightened and met Monica's gaze. "It really couldn't be helped."

"I know." She tried to hide her own disappointment. "Come on into the kitchen and have your dinner. You must be hungry."

"Let me wash up, and I'll be right there." He strode down the hall and disappeared into his bedroom.

Heather's hand slipped into Monica's. "Sunday will still be fun, Mama."

"Of course it will," she answered automatically. "It's only one extra day."

She gave her head a little shake. It *was* only one extra day. These things happened in the business world. The break-in at Solutions—and all the extra work it had caused—was a good example of what could happen to change one's plans. Sometimes a person's job had to take precedence. There were some things a person just couldn't put off, not even for one day, not even for his family.

She knew that was all true, and yet she couldn't stop the hollow, homesick feeling from rushing back. So she did her best to ignore it. Heather was accepting the disappointment. She wasn't about to expect less of herself.

While Daniel ate his dinner, he told Monica and Heather what he could about the story he was covering for the paper. He explained that he couldn't give them particulars because of the nature of the investigation. But he did say it was the biggest thing he'd ever worked on, bar none.

Monica heard the excitement in his voice; she saw it in his eyes. She wanted to be glad for him, but she was oddly disturbed instead.

"Daddy," Heather said at long last, "do you want to know what we did today?"

He looked at his daughter. "Sure, squirt. Tell me all about it."

She launched into one of her energetic monologues, describing every new and strange sight they'd seen that day, from the street hawkers selling imitation designer watches right down to the teenage girl with hot pink colored hair, tattoos and body piercing who they'd seen darting through traffic on her in-line skates. It wasn't long before her parents were both laughing as they saw Chicago through their child's eyes.

Monica's apprehensive feelings dissipated in the warmth of the kitchen. What had she to be concerned about? This was precisely what she'd always dreamed of having. This was the sort of "family moment" that sold greeting cards and made Sunday night movies a hit.

Finally, unable to hide her yawns or her drooping eyes, Heather was sent off to bed. Daniel helped Monica with the last of the dishes, then they went to Heather's bedroom. Monica smoothed the sheet with one hand as she bent over to kiss Heather's forehead.

"Good night, honey."

"Night, Mama."

Daniel stepped to Monica's side, leaned down and kissed his daughter's cheek.

"Night, Daddy."

"Good night, squirt."

Heather yawned. "See ya in the mornin'," she mumbled as she rolled onto her left side.

Before Monica had flipped off the light, Heather was sound asleep.

"Wish I shut down like that," Daniel whispered.

"Me, too."

"I'll probably be up half the night going over the rest of Ed's materials."

"You have more work to do tonight?"

"Yeah. I've got to be ready for that meeting in the morning." He took hold of her hand and led her to the living room. "But it can wait a little while. Let's sit on the balcony and have a glass of wine." He drew her to him. "If I'm lucky, it'll go to your head."

Looking into his eyes, she said, "It always does." She smiled. "So do you."

He kissed her until her knees were weak. He seemed to know that exact moment, for he broke the kiss, then swept her into his arms and carried her the rest of the way to the balcony. Once there, he gently set her on the love seat. "Don't move. I'll get the wine."

Monica closed her eyes and hugged herself, letting the luscious memory of his kisses wash over her. She couldn't doubt he loved her, that he wanted her. And she him. Maybe her moments of anxiety were merely because of pent-up desire. Maybe it was silly to deny them both the pleasure of lovemaking until after the wedding. Why had it seemed so important to her? She couldn't remember now.

She heard his return and looked toward the sliding glass door as he stepped through the opening onto the balcony, a bottle in one hand, two wineglasses in the other.

Her heart quickened at the sight of him. She felt passion unfolding within her like a flower toward the morning sun. She imagined his hands stroking her bare skin and nearly groaned out loud.

"Here you go." He offered her a glass of wine, then sat beside her. "To us." He lifted his goblet in a toast.

"To us."

They sipped wine while continuing to gaze into each other's eyes. Afterward, Daniel slipped an arm around her shoulders. As naturally as day following night, she leaned her head against his chest, and together they stared at the twinkling lights of the city. She could feel the warmth of his skin beneath his shirt. She could hear the beating of his heart, so in tune with her own.

Another wave of wanting washed over her, almost painful in its intensity. It drained her of even enough strength to lift her head and look at him.

How did she tell him she'd changed her mind? How did she tell him she wanted him to make love to her? It should be easy, but she couldn't find the words.

And maybe she was wrong, a small voice reminded her. What message would she be giving Heather if she moved into Daniel's bedroom before the wedding? One day, before Monica was ready for it, Heather would be a young woman, out on her own. Didn't Monica want her daughter to wait until she'd found the man she wanted to love for a lifetime before she gave her body in the most intimate of all actions?

It would be better for Monica to wait, too. She would be setting a better example for their daughter.

But she didn't have to move into his bedroom. She could simply join him there for a few hours. She could simply give herself the warmth and pleasure of his arms. She loved him. They were going to be married in three weeks. What harm could there be? She could return to her own room before morning, before Heather was awake.

"As much as I hate to say this—" Daniel's voice broke into her thoughts "—I'd better get to work. It's almost midnight."

She stirred. "Midnight?" Had they sat there so long?

His arm tightened and he kissed her forehead. "Yes."

Make love to me, Daniel.

He stood, drawing her up with him. "I won't be to bed before three a.m., judging by the papers I need to go over. I've got to be on my toes tomorrow." As he spoke, he walked with her inside and down the hall. They stopped outside her bedroom. "Wish we didn't have to say good-night just yet," he whispered.

Then don't. Stay with me.

He kissed her before turning her by the shoulders and giving her a gentle nudge forward. "Night."

She knew it shouldn't feel as if it were a personal rejection, but it did. She hadn't asked him to make love to her, to stay with her. It was irrational to think he should have read her mind. And yet she believed he should have.

A few minutes later, after putting on her nightshirt and brushing her teeth, she crawled into bed. She lay on her back, staring up at the ceiling, and wondered why loving Daniel made her sometimes as miserable as it made her joyful. Her emotions were often out of control, swinging wildly from the heights of pleasure to the depths of despair.

And there was this physical ache, this need to feel like a woman again. The need for *Daniel* to make her feel like a woman again.

It was a long time before sleep rescued her from her tormenting thoughts.

Chapter Fifteen

Daniel was gone before Monica awakened the next morning. Heather informed her she'd had breakfast with her dad, then handed her mom a note from him.

Monica—Sorry I couldn't wait until you were up. I looked in but you were sleeping soundly. Hope you and Heather have a good day. I'll be home just as soon as I can. I love you. D.

"Well," she said, putting on a more cheerful face than she felt, "what shall we do today?"

Heather shrugged. "I don't know. I sorta wanted to wait for Daddy to do the fun stuff."

She knew just how her daughter felt. She wanted to do the fun stuff with Daniel, too. However, she didn't want to mope around the apartment all day, waiting for him to return. She already felt lonely. She didn't need to be so idle that she was checking her watch every five minutes.

"How about if we go shopping for your new bedroom?" she suggested.

That got the girl's attention. "Really? Today?"

"Sure. Why not?"

"All right!"

Monica ate a quick breakfast, then took her shower and got dressed. An hour later, she and Heather were on their way.

They went to a high-rise shopping mall that contained, it seemed, every imaginable kind of store. They looked at beds and dressers, comforters and sheets, prints for the walls and curtains for the windows, a desk and chair and lamp for studying. Of course, they wouldn't need to buy everything new. Many of Heather's things would be shipped to Chicago from Boise. But it was fun to look.

They stopped to eat lunch, sharing a basket of fish and chips and washing it down with root beer. Then they continued their shopping, this time looking in the clothing stores. A couple of hours later, they returned to the apartment with several bags full—and a balance on Monica's credit card that she knew she would later regret. Both were eager to show Daniel what they'd found.

He wasn't home, but this time there was a message on the answering machine: "Monica, I'm sorry I didn't catch you there. The meeting with Charley and the senator ran longer than I expected, and there are some important details I've got to follow up on today. I don't know how much longer it'll take me. Don't worry if I'm not home for dinner. I'll grab a bite along the way. I miss you both and hope you're having fun. Chill some wine. We'll have a drink on the balcony when I get home."

The call had come in at two o'clock. It was nearly four now.

"Mama?"

"Hmm?

"Do you think Daddy will forget about the zoo tomorrow?"

She glanced at Heather and smiled reassuringly. "Of course he won't forget, honey." She wished she felt as confident as she sounded.

Daniel didn't have any lingering doubts. Someone had tried to murder Ed Tuskin because he'd been getting too close to the truth. He was determined to finish this story for Ed, and hopefully, the young father would be able to read it himself.

As the taxi carried Daniel toward his destination—a deserted warehouse on Elston Avenue—he was aware of the rapid beating of his heart and his heightened sense of perception. The adrenaline was really pumping...

And it felt damn good.

After the Henderson trial, he'd been physically and emotionally drained. He'd thought he'd lost the drive required of a good investigative reporter. But it was back. He knew this could be the biggest story of his entire career. It was stories like this that got a guy a Pulitzer. He could imagine himself, Monica and Heather at his side, as he accepted the award.

"You sure this is the address?" the cabbie asked, drawing Daniel's attention back to the present.

He looked out the window. The multistoried brick warehouse looked as if it was about to crumble. Windows were broken and graffiti was scrawled across the exterior.

"Yeah, this is it."

He paid the driver and got out. As the taxi drove away, leaving him alone on the deserted street, he stood on the sidewalk and stared at the old building.

This was the sort of place Ed had been when he got shot. It could happen to him, too, Daniel thought as he looked around, but his instincts told him this meeting was legit. And his instincts were rarely wrong. He'd learned to depend upon those feelings over the years. He wasn't about to ignore them now. This might be his one and only opportunity to meet with this informant. He couldn't let the chance slip away.

He made his way to the entrance on the south side of the warehouse. It was ajar, just as he'd been told it would be. He slowly pushed it open. The corresponding squeak and groan seemed inordinately loud in his ears, and he clenched his teeth. If someone besides the man he was meeting had heard it, he could be in for trouble.

Trusting the Rourke luck would hold, he slipped through the opening into the darkened warehouse.

Monica and Heather watched two movies on one of the premium cable channels. Daniel still wasn't home by the time the second one ended.

"You'd better go to bed, honey," Monica said as she turned off the television.

"I wanted to see Daddy."

"I know you did, but it looks like he'll be working late again. You'll see him in the morning."

Reluctantly a tired Heather shuffled down the hallway to her room. Monica followed a few minutes later, tucking her in and kissing her good-night.

After her daughter was asleep, Monica wandered from room to room, feeling lonely and wishing Daniel would return. The apartment seemed stark and empty. It was devoid of the sort of items that made a place feel like home. There were no family photos on the mantel or on the walls, no little touches of warmth.

Her sense of aloneness increased when she entered Daniel's bedroom. His king-size bed was neatly made. There were no clothes strewn around. Everything was in its place. It could have been the room of a complete stranger. There were no traces of Daniel in here.

She turned off the overhead light, then lay down on the bed and curled into a ball, her left arm used as a pillow, her right arm flung over her head as if she were hiding from something. She felt like crying, which she knew was silly. And knowing it only made her feel worse.

He hadn't abandoned her, she reminded herself. He was working. His work was important to him. She had always known that about him. She'd learned it years ago…the hard way.

But he'd seemed different in Boise.

Homesickness washed over her once again. She missed her house and her own kitchen and bedroom. She missed Cotton's exuberant affection—wagging tail, lolling tongue, shedding hair and all. She missed her mom and dad. She missed Doug and Terri and Claudia and everyone else at the office.

Most of all, she missed the Daniel she'd fallen in love with in Idaho.

Tears slipped from her eyes, leaving damp tracks on her left cheek, the bridge of her nose and her arm.

It was one-thirty in the morning before Daniel turned his key in his door. A lamp had been left on in the living room. Otherwise, the apartment was dark and still.

He was disappointed, although he shouldn't have

been. He'd hoped Monica would wait up for him. He'd wanted to share what he could about his investigation. He'd wanted to celebrate with her what this story could mean. He'd never had someone else with whom to share this feeling.

He took his briefcase to his office, then looked in on Heather. She was sound asleep, her sheet and blanket a jumbled mess. He wondered what she and her mother had done during the day; whatever it was, it looked like it had worn Heather out.

He moved on to Monica's room. Her bed was empty.

He felt a stab of alarm. He glanced toward the guest bathroom. The door was open, the room dark.

"Monica?" he whispered.

No reply.

He returned to the living room, wondering if she might be out on the balcony and hadn't heard his arrival. She wasn't there.

"Monica?" he said, a bit louder this time.

He checked the kitchen, then headed down the hall a second time.

He found her in his bedroom, asleep on his bed. He switched on the lamp on the nightstand and stared down at her. She looked like an angel, he thought, with her golden curls forming a halo on the bedspread. She wasn't in her nightgown. He suspected she hadn't meant to doze off there.

He leaned over and kissed her forehead.

She opened her eyes. For a moment, she stared at him with a glazed expression, caught between dreams and reality. Then she blinked, and he knew she was fully awake.

"You're back."

"Sorry it's so late. It couldn't be helped."

She glanced at the bedside clock, then sat up, pushing her hair away from her face. "It *is* late. You must be tired." She rose from the bed. "I'd better let you get some sleep."

He stopped her, his hands on her shoulders. "Don't go."

Monica's heart skipped a beat. She wanted to stay more than he would ever know. If he'd asked her last night...

She shook her head, her throat thick with emotion, making it impossible to speak.

"Just for a moment?" he persisted.

She felt the threat of tears again. She didn't want him to know so she pressed her cheek against his chest and wrapped her arms around him.

"Mmm," he whispered as he brushed his mouth over her hair. "You smell good."

She drew in a shaky breath and let it out slowly.

"What did you and Heather do today?"

"Went shopping." She was pleased her reply sounded normal. "Heather bought a new short set to wear to the zoo tomorrow."

"Damn!"

She caught her breath, waiting for him to explain, even though she knew what his expletive meant.

"I can't go tomorrow, Monica." He drew back, searching her face for understanding. "Charley wants a meeting first thing in the morning."

"On Sunday?"

"Everything is heating up fast. We're close to breaking the story. This is the biggest scandal that's hit Chicago since gangsters ran things during Prohibition."

"You promised Heather."

"I know." He released her, then raked the fingers of

his right hand through his hair. "I know I promised. But it can't be helped. Monica, this is a huge opportunity. It could very well be the best story of my career. Opportunities like this don't come along every day."

"I'm not sure that will mean anything to Heather. She's a little girl who's been counting on going to the zoo with her dad."

He muttered another curse under his breath. "I know that."

Monica hugged herself, warding off a chill that had nothing to do with the temperature of the room.

"I'll make it up to her."

I'm sure you'll try, she thought.

"Monica, I *am* sorry." He sounded weary, frustrated, perhaps even a little angry.

She felt exactly the same way. "I know you are, Daniel." She turned away. "Good night."

It was unfair of Monica to make him feel guilty for doing a good job, Daniel told himself several times during the course of the following day.

He would be hard at work, then suddenly he would think of Monica and Heather, and everything would come to a grinding halt. He wondered what they were doing. Were they at the zoo? Eating lunch? Walking along Lake Michigan?

And then he would feel guilty for breaking his promise to Heather.

And then he would feel angry at Monica for making him feel guilty.

They were going to be married soon. They would have a lifetime to spend together. He would take Heather to the zoo. More than once if she wanted. He wasn't always going to be this busy. Once this story was done, he could relax a bit.

In midafternoon, back in his office for the third time that Sunday, Daniel got up from his desk to stretch. He walked over to the window and stared down at the Chicago River. Sunlight glittered over the surface of the waterway. It was a golden summer day to spend outdoors. A cloudless blue sky. A light breeze.

He wondered if Heather liked cotton candy. Or feeding peanuts—or whatever it was they ate—to the giraffes. Had she worn that new short set Monica had told him about? He wondered what color it was.

He checked his watch. He'd better get back to work if he wanted to be home before dark tonight. He didn't want to miss seeing Heather before she went to bed again.

Why did he feel so blasted guilty? All over America husbands and fathers, wives and mothers, sometimes had to work late or go into their offices on their days off. It was just the way it was. The coming of fax machines and e-mail and cell phones and pagers hadn't lessened the workload. They'd increased it. Everybody was working longer days, longer weeks. Daniel couldn't expect to be any different. Especially when he would soon have a family to provide for.

Damn it! Monica should understand all of that. She owned her own business. So why had she looked at him last night with such accusing eyes? As if he'd betrayed her somehow.

He shoved the image from his mind as he returned to his desk. He had to concentrate on his work. Monica was just going to have to understand.

The nation's oldest zoo, Lincoln Park Zoo featured naturalistic exhibits for its nineteen hundred mammals, birds and reptiles. Heather seemed to particularly enjoy the big cats and the koala bears. Monica favored the exotic birds.

But no matter what they were doing, no matter how wonderful Lincoln Park and the animals, no matter how perfect the weather, a corner of Monica's mind—or was it a corner of her heart?—kept reminding her that Daniel's work was more important to him than his promise to Heather.

In the afternoon, they returned, once again, to an empty apartment. No sign of Daniel. No message on the answering machine. Monica wavered between heartache and anger, neither one of which she wanted Heather to see.

While her daughter plopped herself down in front of the television, Monica went to the kitchen to prepare the two of them a light evening meal. She didn't fix extra this time. She didn't care if Daniel came home starved to death. He could jolly well fix his own dinner. She'd be darned if she was going to cook for him.

Well, that settled it, she thought. She was more furious than hurt. And once she recognized her feelings, she longed to vent them. Since Daniel wasn't around to receive the brunt of it, she took it out on the kitchen, banging dishes and pots and slamming drawers and cupboard doors.

In Boise, Daniel had acted as if he wanted them to be a family. He'd seemed to enjoy spending time with Monica and Heather. He'd indicated he wanted something different from what he'd had these past eleven years. But now she couldn't be sure he felt that way. He'd been called back to Chicago because of an emergency. Was this a temporary situation or would it always be this way?

She choked on an unexpected sob. She was scared. She would rather fly around the world twice than see them coming apart at the seams a second time.

"Mama! Come quick!"

Responding to the urgency in Heather's voice, Monica rushed from the kitchen to the living room.

"Look!" Heather pointed toward the television. "It's Daddy."

Indeed it was. A still photo of Daniel filled the big-screen TV.

"Turn up the sound, honey."

Heather obliged, and the newsreader's voice filled the room. "Charles Cooper had no comment when asked what prompted Daniel Rourke's return to Chicago recently, but according to one source, the seasoned reporter will soon have his byline once again in the paper. The general opinion on the street seems to be his return will be welcomed by the reading public." A film clip followed, the reporter interviewing people on the street. "He's one of the best, one of the few honest guys in the media, if you ask me," one man said. "Oh, I never missed a Daniel Rourke article when he was writing for the paper," a twenty-something woman announced, "and I couldn't put down his book about the Henderson case. He's pretty cute, too." "The morning paper hasn't been the same without him," a grandmotherly type said as she stared seriously toward the camera.

"And so," the newsreader continued, "we say, welcome back, Daniel Rourke. Chicago has missed you." The newscast continued with sports.

Chicago has missed you.

Heather turned down the sound again. "Wow! That was neat. Wasn't it, Mama?"

We miss you, too, Daniel.

"Mama?"

She shook off her thoughts. "Yes, honey, it was cool. You'll have to tell your dad you saw it."

If he gets home in time, she silently added.

As it turned out, Daniel did make it home before Heather went to bed, but he was too keyed up to pay much attention to what she was telling him.

Not long before he'd left the newspaper office, he'd received what he believed to be the break of his lifetime. The last piece of the puzzle had fallen into place. The story was ready to go, with just some minor tweaking. Charley was waiting for him to send the final draft to him via computer modem just as soon as he had it finished.

"As long as they don't get wind of the real story until tomorrow," he told Monica, "I don't care what they say about me on TV."

"Don't you?"

He frowned at her odd question. "*No,* I don't."

She shrugged and left the living room.

He thought about following her, then turned back to Heather who was still seated on the couch, her legs curled beneath her. "I've got some work to do, squirt. How about if you tell me about the zoo in the morning?"

"Whatever."

For a second, he thought she sounded like her mother.

What was wrong with the two of them? Didn't they understand how important this was?

Feeling out of sorts, he headed for the office next to his bedroom. He closed the door behind him, then sat down at his desk, turned on the computer, and after it booted up, slipped the floppy disk into the disk drive.

Nearly three hours later, he picked up the phone and called his editor. "Check your e-mail, Charley," he said without wasting time for a greeting. "I just sent it over to you. Sorry it took a little longer than I thought it would."

"It's still in time to make the morning edition." Charley's voice was riddled with the same excitement and anticipation Daniel had been feeling. "Listen, Rourke, you'd better plan to be at the paper first thing in the morning. The television media's gonna be swarming all over this place, looking to talk to you. And I imagine there'll be a few government officials who'll want a piece of your time, too."

He grinned. "Yeah, I just bet they will."

"Well, go celebrate with that fiancée of yours. How 'bout the three of us have dinner together tomorrow night? I'd like to meet this gal who stole your heart."

"Make it four of us and you're on."

"Four?"

"My daughter will be with us."

"Okay, four it is. I'll make reservations." There was a pause, then, "Rourke, great job. I mean it."

"Thanks. See you in the morning."

He hung up the phone. Celebrating sounded good. He'd like nothing better than to snuggle up with Monica and tell her everything about the story. Now that it was written and ready to go to press, he wouldn't have to hold anything back. Once he told her, she would understand why this had all been so important.

Only, when he emerged from his office, he found he was once again too late. Monica and Heather had both gone to bed.

Chapter Sixteen

Monica was awakened at five-thirty by the ringing of the telephone. She blinked her eyes to make certain she'd seen the time correctly. She had.

She rolled over and covered her head with her pillow. Who would be calling Daniel this early in the morning? Curse them!

She hadn't slept well, and she was exhausted. There was this hard knot in the pit of her stomach that wouldn't go away; that hollow feeling in her chest was still there, too.

The phone rang again, just twice this time before Daniel picked it up.

She jerked the pillow from her face and stared upward. The first fingers of daylight were inching across the ceiling. She wondered what time Daniel had gone to bed. He'd been working, his door closed, when she and Heather gave up waiting and retired to their own rooms.

"Daniel," she whispered, "what's happening to us?"

Again the phone rang, this time once.

What on earth?

She got out of bed and hurried to the door. She opened it and peeked into the hall, looking toward his bedroom. There was a light under his door, and she could hear his muffled voice, although she couldn't make out what he was saying.

His voice rose sharply. "I said I'll call you later." The sound of the receiver slamming into its cradle was unmistakable.

A moment later, his door flew open, crashing against the wall. He strode down the hall, wearing pajama bottoms, his chest and feet bare, his hair tousled. He was muttering beneath his breath. Then he saw her and stopped.

"What's wrong?" she asked.

By turns, he looked irritated, surprised, then bemused. Finally he grinned sheepishly and admitted, "Nothing, except I wanted to sleep a bit longer."

"Who was on the phone?"

"A congressman, the mayor's assistant and a television reporter. In that order. The story's in today's paper. Apparently I've struck a few nerves." He grabbed her suddenly by the shoulders and gave her a quick kiss. When he released her, he said, "I'll get the paper." Then he headed for the front door, his footsteps lighter than they'd been before.

A short while later, Monica sat at the kitchen table, sipping her coffee and reading the article that had consumed Daniel from almost the moment they'd arrived in Chicago. At last, she understood what he'd been trying to tell her. If Daniel Rourke had been well-known before, he would be doubly so now. She looked over at him.

Still in his pajama bottoms, he leaned against the island counter, his arms folded over his chest, his ankles crossed. He wore what could only be described as a Cheshire cat grin.

"Charley wants to take us out to dinner tonight to celebrate," he told her. "He's really looking forward to meeting you."

"What about Heather?"

"Her, too. Get gussied up, as my dad used to say. I'm going to make sure Charley take us someplace fancy and pricey." His smile broadened. "*Very* pricey. He owes me after the last few days."

"I can see why he brought you back to do this story. You did an excellent job."

"Ed deserves a lot of the credit. I just pulled it all together in his absence. That's why we're sharing the byline. I couldn't have done it without all the legwork he did before I got involved."

"How is he? Ed, I mean."

Daniel pushed off from the counter. "Lots better. The doctors are amazed. He's awake and talking some. I'll bet his wife is reading him the article right now. I'm going by to see him later today."

A new thought occurred to her. "Was it an accident that he was shot? Or did it have to do with this investigation?"

"We'll probably never know."

"And you, Daniel? Are you in danger?"

A small frown pulled his eyebrows toward one another. "I could have been." He shrugged and the frown vanished. "But not now that it's all been made public. My guess is there'll be some arrests made within a day or two. This wasn't news to the police. They've been after these guys. Especially the cops on the take.''

She pondered this for a few moments.

''Listen,'' he said, breaking into her thoughts, ''I'd better get into the shower and go to the office. Charley's expecting me soon. I'll put the phone in my bedroom back on the hook.''

She glanced toward the telephone on the kitchen wall. ''I wondered why it was so quiet.''

''You might want to turn the ringer down and let the machine screen calls. I suspect there'll be a few people trying to track me down here.'' He bent over and kissed her forehead. ''I'm off to the shower.''

She listened to him whistling softly as he strode down the hall. When she heard his door close behind him, she lowered her gaze to the newspaper again.

It was a brilliant piece. Several brilliant pieces actually. There were photos and charts and even a copy of an actual letter that implicated some well-known names. Well-known even to a woman from Idaho. Any reporter would have been proud to write this story, but it was Daniel who had done it. She wanted to share his pride in what he'd accomplished, but she was unable to shake her sense of overwhelming dread.

''Daniel Rourke is back, and he's better than ever,'' Charley Cooper said as he looked into the camera. ''And we've got him.''

''Mama?'' Heather tugged on Monica's sleeve. ''Is Daddy ever going to have time to do stuff with us?''

Monica shifted her gaze from the television and the six o'clock newscast to her daughter who was seated beside her on the sofa. She tried to think of something comforting to say, but her mind was a blank.

Heather frowned. ''I liked it better at home. In Boise. He wanted to be with us then.''

She put her arm around her child's shoulders and gave her a squeeze. ''This will all be over soon. No one will even remember it a week from now.'' She knew she was lying. She knew it wouldn't be over by then. Maybe it would never be over. Daniel was a celebrity.

Heather saw through the lie. ''No, it won't,'' she mumbled. Then she picked up the remote control and changed the channel just as the television flashed another photo of her father.

Heather's words stayed with Monica as she finished getting ready for their dinner out on the town. She stared at her reflection in the bathroom mirror while brushing her hair and wondered if Daniel cared that his daughter was feeling so left out.

It wasn't easy, taking a child from her home, friends and extended family and plopping her down in a strange environment. Perhaps Heather's expectations were a trifle unrealistic, but Daniel should have made an effort to spend more time with her.

But this story—and his career—had come first.

She'd been down this road before.

''I'm home!''

The sound of Daniel's voice caused her heart to jump, and she was filled with an odd mixture of pleasure and sorrow. She heard Heather greet him, knew the two of them exchanged a hug.

Daniel loved Heather. He loved Monica, too. She believed it with all her heart, knew it to be true. But was it enough? She'd thought love was *always* enough. Now she wasn't so sure.

''Hi, sweetheart.''

She turned toward the bathroom door.

He was holding a bouquet of red roses. "They didn't have any calla lilies. These will have to do."

She smiled. "They're beautiful."

"So are you." He stepped into the room, dropped the roses on the counter, then pulled Monica close for a kiss. When their lips parted, he said, "You wouldn't believe my day."

"Maybe we should stay home. Just spend the evening together, the three of us."

He raised his eyebrows. "Are you kidding? This is a night to spend on the town. Besides, Charley's eager to meet you and Heather." He looked at his watch. "I'd better get changed if we want to arrive at the restaurant on time." He kissed her on the cheek, then strode down the hall to his bedroom.

Forty minutes later, Daniel ushered his fiancée and daughter into the restaurant. Charley was waiting for them at their table. Daniel performed the introductions, then they were all seated.

It didn't take Monica long to decide she could like Charley. Though no more than ordinary in appearance— gray hair, glasses, a round, slightly pudgy face—the fif-tyish Charley Cooper had an engaging smile and a friendly laugh. He looked every bit the newspaper editor.

It was obvious he was enormously proud of his star reporter. "You can't imagine how much we've missed Daniel at the paper. I'm damn glad he's back with us. I can tell you that."

The champagne Charley had ordered arrived at that moment. Glasses were filled all around. Heather was served a Shirley Temple. Then Charley toasted Daniel's success.

Before they'd set their glasses down, Charley launched into a detailed report of what he anticipated would transpire over the next few days. There would be more television interviews, of course, and he'd already had requests for Daniel to appear on some nationally syndicated talk shows. "You might need to go to New York in the next couple of weeks. Maybe sooner."

Monica wasn't so sure she could like Charley Cooper, after all.

She glanced expectantly toward Daniel, waiting for him to remind his editor why he couldn't go to New York. Instead he peppered Charley with questions and comments about which talk shows it would be best to appear on, what follow-up articles would be necessary and how soon, and more.

It seemed he'd forgotten the little matter of his own wedding.

On the drive home from the restaurant, Daniel could feel the tension emanating from Monica. She hadn't enjoyed herself tonight as he'd expected her to. He'd noticed that her smile hadn't ever reached her eyes. He wanted to ask her what was wrong, but he decided to wait until they were back to the apartment.

He settled for an attempt at small talk. "My steak was delicious. How was your salmon?"

"Good."

"You should have tried that dessert."

No response.

"Heather, how about you? Did you like your dinner?"

"It was okay."

To Monica again: "It's a nice restaurant. We'll go back some time if you'd like to."

"If that's what you want."

Hmm. ''Charley was taken with both you and Heather. I could tell.''

''He seems nice.'' Monica turned her head to look out the window, effectively using body language to stop further conversation.

So much for small talk.

By the time they reached the high-rise, Heather had fallen asleep in the back seat. Daniel carried her up to the apartment and into her bedroom. She hardly stirred, waking just enough for Monica to help get her out of her party dress and into her nightclothes. Both parents kissed the girl good-night, then left the bedroom at the same time, Monica leading the way.

She went straight toward her own room.

''Monica, wait.'' He caught her gently by the arm.

She turned toward him. ''I'm tired, Daniel. I'm going to bed.''

''What's the matter?''

Her eyes widened. ''You really don't know, do you?''

He shrugged, mystified by her mood.

She pulled free of his hand. ''Do you suppose your interviews in New York will get in the way of our wedding or the little matter of our honeymoon?''

''Is that what this is about? Did you really think I'd forgotten?''

She ignored his questions and asked one of her own. ''Do you know how little time you've spent with us since we got to Chicago?''

''It couldn't be helped, and you know it.'' He felt his temper rising. Why was she being difficult and temperamental, tonight of all nights? They were supposed to be celebrating, and instead he perceived a fight coming on.

"What about the next story, Daniel? Can *it* be helped?" She turned and marched into her bedroom.

He followed right after her before she could close the door in his face. "I don't understand any of this. I thought you'd be glad for me."

"Oh, I'm glad for you." She removed her earrings and dropped them onto the dresser before facing him once again. "You're a huge success. Everyone knows who you are. You're on the evening news. Your photo and byline are in the newspaper. You will no doubt get another blockbuster book out of this mess when it's all over. But that could take years, couldn't it, by the time it moves through the courts and you've written your countless articles on all the defendants and suspects and witnesses. And when, in between all that, do you intend to spend any time with Heather?"

He swore. "We've been in Chicago less than a week. I'll take her to the damn zoo soon."

"This isn't about the zoo. She just wants to be with you. Do you know what she said to me today? She said she liked it better in Boise because you wanted to spend time with us when we were there."

He felt those words like an upper cut to the chin, but he shoved aside the guilt, letting his anger grow hotter. "What do you *want* from me? I'm a reporter. This is my *job.*"

"Lots of people have jobs," she retorted, her eyes flashing, "and they don't forget what's really important. Heather won't be a little girl much longer. She'll be grown in an instant, and you won't even know your own daughter."

"That's ridiculous. I'm not ignoring Heather. You're overreacting." He swore again. "There's no talking to you when you're like this." He strode out of the room.

The instant the door closed behind Daniel, Monica sank onto the bed, her knees too weak to hold her up. She was shaking all over.

As if it was yesterday, their fights from years ago replayed in her mind, mingling with the one that had just occurred, magnifying this one many times over.

She lay down, covering her face with her hands as she swallowed a sob.

He hadn't changed. And neither had she. They wanted different things. Too different.

She rolled onto her stomach and wept into her pillow.

Three days later, Monica and Heather went to Navy Pier, both of them hoping a few rides and other amusements might cheer them up. The apartment had been glum for days. Monica had held out a slim hope that she and Daniel could talk reasonably about their argument and what had caused it. But he'd been gone from dawn to long after dark every day. She thought he might be avoiding her.

Mother and daughter tried to have a good time that afternoon. They rode the Ferris Wheel and the merry-go-round. They walked through the indoor tropical gardens and browsed the small shops. They ate junk food— popcorn, candied apples, white chocolate and macadamia nut cookies, snow cones. But after a couple of hours, it was clear the outing had done little to improve their moods. So they headed back to the apartment.

They hadn't gone far before they saw a bus across the street, parked while passengers boarded. And on the side of that bus was Daniel's picture with the words: Daniel Rourke. He's Back...And Better Than Ever!

"I want to go home, Mama." Heather's voice cracked. "To our house. I don't like it here."

A sick knot formed in Monica's stomach. It was over. It couldn't work. Maybe she was unreasonable. Maybe she was asking too much of him. But she couldn't help it. She wanted more than this. More than he was willing or able to give.

She squeezed Heather's hand. ''All right, honey. We'll go home.''

By the time they reached the apartment, Monica's chest felt as if it were being crushed beneath an enormous weight. She wanted to give in to tears, to let herself wallow in her own broken heart, in her own broken dreams. But for Heather's sake, she didn't. It would be bad enough when she told Daniel she was calling off the wedding.

She went into the kitchen to phone the airline for flight times and availability. The message light was blinking on the answering machine. She punched the button.

''Monica? It's me. I'm calling from my cell phone on the way to the airport. I came home but you were out. I've got to go to New York overnight. I'll be back about six tomorrow evening. Listen, we need to talk. I'm sorry about the other night. And I'm sorry I've been gone so much. I've been thinking and... Oh, heck. I don't want to do this on the machine. I need to say it in person. We'll talk tomorrow night. I love you, sweetheart. Tell Heather I love her, too.''

Click.

Beep.

It was a while before she realized there were tears streaming down her cheeks.

''I love you, too, Daniel.''

She picked up the phone and dialed reservations.

                    *   *   *

Daniel opened the door to his apartment. "Hey, anybody home?" he called out.

He was met with silence.

It wasn't even eight o'clock yet. Surely they weren't in bed already. He went to check. There was no sign of either of them. Their beds were neatly made, nothing on the dressers. The rooms looked strangely sterile.

He frowned as he headed toward the kitchen. Hadn't Monica received his phone message yesterday, telling her when he would be home?

He was eager to see her, eager to talk. When he'd told her in the message that he'd been thinking, it had been an understatement. He'd faced some harsh facts about himself over the past few days, and he...

He stopped suddenly, his eyes focused on a slip of paper on the counter beside the answering machine. And lying on top of it was the diamond engagement ring he'd given Monica.

With his heart thudding, he picked up the note and began to read:

Daniel,
On Friday, Heather and I took a walk along the shores of Lake Michigan. You weren't with us. On Saturday, we went shopping, just the two of us. On Sunday, Heather and I went to the zoo, but you were still absent. On Monday, we stayed in the apartment and watched television and the reports about your story. We saw you on the news. On Tuesday, we went back to the lake. On Wednesday, we visited the Navy Pier. We saw your picture on the side of a bus. On Thursday, we flew home.

We missed you, Daniel. I'm taking Heather back to Boise where we both belong. I thought love was enough. I was wrong. I'm sorry.

Monica

Chapter Seventeen

"Monica dear," Ellen Fletcher said, concern lacing her voice, "you must eat. You are positively wasting away."

The two of them were having their regular one o'clock Monday lunch at their favorite bistro. Just as if everything were normal. Just as if Monica's heart hadn't been shattered into a thousand tiny pieces.

Monica gave her head a small shake while pushing the food around her plate with her fork.

"You've been back from Chicago ten days," her mother continued, "and I'll bet you've lost as many pounds."

"I'm not hungry, Mom."

Ellen reached across the table and took hold of Monica's hand. "Look at me."

She obeyed the stern command.

"Have you returned Daniel's calls?"

"No." The word almost wouldn't come out over the lump in her throat.

"Monica, I've tried not to interfere, but—"

"Then don't interfere."

"But, dear, what if—"

"*Don't,* Mom."

Ellen released a deep sigh while Monica gently but firmly withdrew her hand from her mother's grasp.

Several minutes of strained silence passed before Monica whispered, "I don't want to talk about it. I don't want to *think* about it. It won't change anything. Heather is unhappy, and so am I." She met her mother's gaze. "I made a terrible mistake telling him about Heather. I should have left well enough alone. I thought this would be a good thing for her, but I was wrong. I wanted to do what was right, and all I did was hurt my daughter." She released a ragged breath, then added, "And myself."

Ellen remained silent.

"It's so hard, Mom. I didn't know it could hurt this bad."

"Give yourself time."

At the moment, she didn't think time would help.

"Maybe you and Heather should take a little vacation. Maybe you could visit that friend of yours in Alaska. Alaska must be gorgeous this time of year."

Monica looked out the window. A little vacation... She'd thought she would be on her honeymoon next week.

Abruptly she stood. "I'd better get back to the office."

Her mother rose, too.

"I'm not going to wallow in self-pity any longer," she announced. "Everyone at the office is tiptoeing around, being so careful what they say or how they look at me. It's horrible, and it's time I put a stop to it.''

"You can't expect to get over something like this overnight.''

"No, but I don't have to be morbid about it, either.''

It felt good to say that. It felt good to believe it.

She'd loved unwisely, but she would get over it. She'd survived before. She would survive again.

She hooked arms with Ellen as they left the bistro.

Even though the temperature had soared into the high nineties on this mid-July afternoon, they walked slowly, pausing several times to admire dresses and jewelry in shop windows. Neither of them was truly interested in what they saw, but both pretended to be for the sake of the other.

At last they arrived at Monica's office building. They stopped on the sidewalk and exchanged an embrace.

"Don't worry about me,'' Monica said in her mother's ear. "I'm going to be okay.''

"Of course you will.''

They drew apart. Ellen's eyes glittered with unshed tears. Monica knew hers must look the same.

"Come for dinner tomorrow night. Your father is working on a new birdhouse. I'm sure Heather would love to see it.''

Monica shrugged. "I'll have to let you know.''

Her mother didn't push. "All right, dear.'' She touched Monica's cheek. "Call me.''

"Thanks, Mom.''

She watched Ellen walk toward the entrance to the parking garage, then she pushed open the big glass door and entered the office building. A moment later, in the elevator, she once again had to fight the urge to give in to a flood of tears. Her new resolve to be positive and not to feel sorry for herself was already flagging.

She managed to regain fragile control over her emotions before the elevator stopped at her floor.

Terri looked up, a smile of welcome on her face. The smile immediately vanished when she recognized Monica. "Ms. Fletcher, there's someone waiting in—"

"Not now, Terri," she said, her hand raised like a traffic cop. She needed to get to her office and close the door. She didn't want witnesses when she fell apart.

She walked down the hall with as much decorum as she could muster. She kept her gaze fastened on the floor just a few feet in front of her, taking no chance of making eye contact with anyone. She didn't want to hear how sorry someone was. She just wanted to stop hurting.

None too soon, she dashed through the doorway into her office, shutting herself in, then pressed her forehead against the door.

Why did it have to hurt so much?

She drew in a deep breath, let it out, straightened and turned.

And then she gasped.

Daniel was standing beside her desk.

"Hello, Monica."

He thought she looked too thin. There were dark circles under her eyes. Her face was pale and wan. She looked like she was holding on by a thread.

And it was all his fault.

"You never returned my calls," he said as he took a step toward her.

"I couldn't. It wouldn't serve any purpose. We can't change who we are."

"I don't believe that." He motioned toward a chair. "Will you sit down? I've got a lot to tell you."

If possible, she seemed to grow more pale.

"Please, Monica."

He waited, afraid to hope she would do as he'd asked. He couldn't blame her if she marched out of the office without hearing what he'd come to say.

He didn't realize he'd been holding his breath until she moved to sit down. He let the air out of his lungs, then followed to sit near her. She didn't look at him. Instead she stared down at her hands, clenched tightly in her lap.

Don't let me blow this chance, he thought before he said, "I've been busy since you left Chicago." It was the wrong thing to say. He'd been busy while she was there, too.

She didn't act as if she'd heard him.

He tried again. "You were right about me, Monica. I got swept up in the rat race again. I guess it's like a drug for me. I hadn't realized." He touched the back of her hand with his fingertips. "I forgot what was most important."

She stiffened but didn't pull away.

"I'm not ever going to forget again. I love you, and I don't want to lose you."

"Oh, Daniel," she whispered. "Don't."

"I gave Charley my notice."

He heard her surprised intake of breath. She looked up at him, her gaze questioning, hesitant, doubtful.

"I moved out of the apartment. My things are being shipped to Boise as we speak. I had an interview this morning for a columnist position with the *Boise Herald*. No travel to speak of. Decent hours. Reasonable salary. I got the job. When I start is up to you."

"To me?"

He nodded, at the same time wondering if she could tell how scared he was. "Yeah. I can start tomorrow…" He paused briefly, then continued, "Or I can start when we get back from our honeymoon."

Twin tears slid down her cheeks. "What if you aren't happy in Boise? Or with me? I just want a simple life with simple pleasures. A family to love and be loved by. Nothing too exciting or glamorous. What if that isn't enough for you, Daniel? You've always wanted so much more."

"I'll be happy here. It'll be enough. *You'll* be enough." He took hold of her hands, pressing them between his own as he leaned forward in his chair. "I discovered there wasn't anything in Chicago for me after you and Heather left. I don't want to live on that treadmill anymore, Monica. Deep down I knew that when I came here last spring. I just forgot for a while. Then you left and I remembered. So I got off of it. Off the treadmill. I've come home. For good. Whether you'll take me back or not, I'm here to stay." He lowered his voice. "But I'm hoping and praying you'll take me back."

She stared at him. Not blinking. Not even seeming to breathe. Just staring.

"You don't have any reason to believe me. I know that. But I swear to you I'll be a devoted husband and father. I made it real clear to my new editor. I'll turn in my columns, just like I was hired to do. The rest of my time is my own, and it will belong to my family."

If she didn't say something soon, he thought he'd go crazy. There wasn't anything else in this world that mattered as much to him as her answer.

Finally, an eternity later, she spoke, her voice uncertain. "I was always such a dreamer. Always wanting happily ever after. Perfect endings and all that. You used to tease me about it. Remember?'' She swallowed. ''Am I dreaming now, Daniel?''

''No.''

Her smile was tremulous. ''Then I suppose the church might still be available on Saturday. And I just happen to know where we can find a flower girl and a wedding gown.''

The instant the words were out of her mouth, he pulled her up from her chair and crushed her in his embrace. He kissed her hungrily, not trying to hide the desperation he'd been feeling.

He'd been given another chance.

The wedding was everything a bride could want, despite all the last-minute preparations.

Surrounded by family and friends, Monica and Daniel exchanged their vows, promising to love and to cherish each other for the rest of their lives. Standing with them, Heather beamed, reflecting the joy they all felt.

At the reception that followed, the bride and groom were toasted and wished many blessings and years together. Then they danced while all their loved ones watched and applauded. Finally they slipped away, driving off in a car that proudly proclaimed Just Married! on three sides and trailed crepe paper streamers from the antenna and rear bumper.

It was a day more wonderful than any dream.

Monica stood in the luxurious bathroom of the elegant honeymoon suite, staring at her reflection in the mirror. She was wearing a white satin negligee, a garment that was at the same time demure and provocative. Her hair fell loose over her shoulders, the way Daniel liked it best.

She pressed both hands against her stomach in an attempt to quell the fluttering therein. She was nervous. She felt as shy and uncertain as a virgin.

But perhaps she was more nervous because she *wasn't* that innocent virgin. Long ago, she'd been Daniel's lover. She'd known his touch. She'd tasted his kisses and surrendered to the sweet ecstasy of his lovemaking. Would he find her as desirable now as he had then?

Her gaze flicked to the door, and her jitters faded away. Daniel was waiting for her in the other room. She was his wife. He was her husband. He loved her. She had nothing to be nervous about. It seemed too wonderful to be believed, and yet it was true.

Drawing a deep breath, she opened the bathroom door.

An unexpected sight awaited her. Candles of every shape, color and size flickered on tables, nightstands, dresser and TV. A single calla lily, pale pink in color, lay on a pillow at the head of the king-size bed.

Her groom stood on the far side of the room. The look he gave her was like a physical caress. The butterflies started fluttering again. This time from anticipation.

Without breaking his gaze from hers, Daniel pressed a button on the stereo. A heartbeat later, the room was filled with music. And the words of the song brought tears to her eyes.

"Beautiful dreamer, queen of my song, List while I woo thee with soft melody; Gone are the cares of life's busy throng, Beautiful dreamer, awake unto me!"

Did he move first or did she? She couldn't be sure. She only knew they were suddenly standing together in the center of the room, her arms around his waist, the palms of his hands cradling her face.

"You're *my* beautiful dreamer."

She smiled. His wonderful gray eyes stared deeply into hers, and it seemed to Monica that he had touched her heart.

"Thank you," he said, his voice deep and low. "Thank you for making me a part of your dreams."

Was it possible to die of too much happiness?

She rose on tiptoe. He lowered his head. Their lips met. A slow burn began inside her, a fire Monica knew only her husband could quench.

Daniel, in the role of her knight in shining armor, swept her feet off the floor and carried her to the bed. He laid her beside the calla lily, and the way he looked at her made her feel as beautiful as her favorite flower. With slow, deliberate movements, he removed the nightgown she had donned such a short time ago. With his caress and his kisses, he silently declared his adoration.

The lovemaking that followed was everything she had imagined...and more.

The candles had burned low. Some had sputtered and died. The blanket and top sheet were tangled and twisted. Monica lay in the circle of Daniel's arms, her head resting on his shoulder, her hair fanning out across the sheets.

The last hour of slow, tender, ecstatic lovemaking had satiated, for now, his physical desire. He knew he would want to make love to her again. And often. But for now he was content to simply hold her near and feel her heart beating in unison with his own.

Daniel had traveled the world. He had visited countless countries, experienced many different cultures. He had met with presidents and kings and religious leaders. He had interviewed the famous and the infamous, the beautiful and the grotesque. He had seen the best and the worst in humankind. He had acquired wealth, won awards and garnered the respect of his peers. It seemed he had achieved everything he'd set out to do.

He drew Monica closer. He kissed the tip of her nose. She murmured sleepily but didn't open her eyes.

He smiled, contented.

Yes, he'd done many things. He'd been successful in numerous ways. But it had taken him a lot of years— too many years—to learn one simple truth...

None of it meant anything without the love of his hometown girl.

*　*　*　*　*

Look for Robin Lee Hatcher's next wonderful book, TAKING CARE OF THE TWINS, coming this July from Silhouette Special Edition.

If you enjoyed what you just read,
then we've got an offer you can't resist!

Take 2 bestselling love stories FREE!
Plus get a FREE surprise gift!

Clip this page and mail it to Silhouette Reader Service™

IN U.S.A.
3010 Walden Ave.
P.O. Box 1867
Buffalo, N.Y. 14240-1867

IN CANADA
P.O. Box 609
Fort Erie, Ontario
L2A 5X3

YES! Please send me 2 free Silhouette Special Edition® novels and my free surprise gift. Then send me 6 brand-new novels every month, which I will receive months before they're available in stores. In the U.S.A., bill me at the bargain price of $3.57 plus 25¢ delivery per book and applicable sales tax, if any*. In Canada, bill me at the bargain price of $3.96 plus 25¢ delivery per book and applicable taxes**. That's the complete price and a savings of over 10% off the cover prices—what a great deal! I understand that accepting the 2 free books and gift places me under no obligation ever to buy any books. I can always return a shipment and cancel at any time. Even if I never buy another book from Silhouette, the 2 free books and gift are mine to keep forever. So why not take us up on our invitation. You'll be glad you did!

235 SEN CNFD
335 SEN CNFE

Name	(PLEASE PRINT)	
Address	Apt.#	
City	State/Prov.	Zip/Postal Code

* Terms and prices subject to change without notice. Sales tax applicable in N.Y.
** Canadian residents will be charged applicable provincial taxes and GST.
   All orders subject to approval. Offer limited to one per household.
   ® are registered trademarks of Harlequin Enterprises Limited.

SPED99   ©1998 Harlequin Enterprises Limited

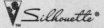

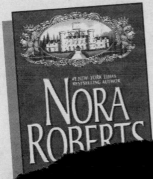

Silhouette®

SPECIAL EDITION®

COMING NEXT MONTH

#1231 DREAM BRIDE—Susan Mallery
That Special Woman!/Brides of Bradley House
According to family legend, Chloe Wright was destined to dream of her future husband on her twenty-fifth birthday. The self-proclaimed pragmatist didn't believe in fairy tales…until enigmatic Arizona Smith mysteriously entered Chloe's life—and passionately swept her off her feet.

#1232 THE PERFECT NEIGHBOR—Nora Roberts
The MacGregors
Brooding loner Preston McQuinn was determined never to love again. But he could hardly resist his vivacious neighbor Cybil Campbell, who was determined to win his stubborn heart. Would the matchmaking Daniel MacGregor see his granddaughter happily married to the man she adored?

#1233 HUSBAND IN TRAINING—Christine Rimmer
Nick DeSalvo wanted to trade in his bachelor ways for his very own family. And who better than Jenny Brown—his best friend's nurturing widow—to give him lessons on how to be a model husband? But how long would it take the smitten, reformed heartbreaker to realize he wanted *Jenny* as his wife?

#1234 THE COWBOY AND HIS WAYWARD BRIDE—Sherryl Woods
And Baby Makes Three: The Next Generation
Rancher Harlan Patrick Adams was fit to be tied! The only woman who'd ever mattered to him had secretly given birth to *his* baby girl. And he couldn't bear to be apart from his family for another second. Could the driven father convince fiercely independent Laurie Jensen to be his bride?

#1235 MARRYING AN OLDER MAN—Arlene James
She was young, innocent and madly in love with her much older boss.
_____ Moncton enticed him, gorgeous
_____ ng guy. But she
_____ isle!